NASHUA'S CHOICE

DONNA COOK

*To Kami,
What would you choose?
Donna Cook*

To Pam:
That could you
close for

Also by Donna Cook:

Gift of the Phoenix
The Lost Branch

Copyright © 2013 Donna Cook

All rights reserved. No part of this book may be used or reproduced in whole or in part, in any manner whatsoever without written permission from the publisher, except in the case of brief quotations embodied in critical articles or reviews.

Published by Penrose House Press, LLC
United States of America
www.penrosehousepress.com

www.donnacookauthor.com

ISBN 978-0-9882089-5-7

Printed in the United States of America

Acknowledgments

My everlasting thanks to my editor and dear friend, Elyse Martin. The one whose opinion matters most.

Thanks to my fellow writers and critical beta readers, Louise Berlin, Debra Anne Bishop, Dynisha Smith, Nicole Green, and Kira McCain. Your diligence and support are invaluable.

Thanks to my boys for their enthusiasm and faith.

To my stepdaughters for being cool like that.

To my parents, for giving me life and courage.

And to my husband, Kevin, who knows how to keep my feet on the ground while giving wings to my dreams.

For my mother, Barbara,
for being the first to believe.

Nashua's Choice

One

The stone amphitheater, draped in magical vines and drenched in sunshine, reverberates with the Song of Strength. Few citizens have come for the song today. Nashua finds it difficult to sing with her usual care, distracted by anticipation. There will be no evening songs today, just this last midday song. They will spend the rest of the day gathering, preparing, anticipating, celebrating. After centuries of waiting, there are only a few hours to go. The Phoenix is coming at last.

Her enchanted pewter horn necklace offers its last as Nashua finishes the song. The vibrating pulse of the amphitheater stills and the magic disappears into the air like a feathered whiff of smoke. It lingers in the heart of the listeners though. They slowly gather themselves and filter out of the opening to the rear. Nashua follows them into the cobbled courtyard. Citizens are filing out of the amphitheaters for the Song of Comfort, the Song of Patience, the Song of Openness, and all the rest. Nashua, like the other

Chanters, stays by the entrance to her amphitheater while she waits for the courtyard to clear. People gradually make their way through the Great Gate, on their way back to their homes in the city or perhaps in the nearby hills. A few recognize one another and stop to visit quietly. Fountains and flowering bushes lend to the tranquility of this place.

Nashua usually enjoys this moment, watching the faces of their patrons and seeing the inner glow that comes from what they've just experienced. So unlike the heavy expressions frequently seen before the songs begin. This day is different however. This day she is in a hurry. She checks the sky. The sun is still rising but nearing its crest. How long the day has been! It seems the sun will never set. Perhaps she needs the Song of Patience herself.

Villaciti Cantori is a sprawling, walled compound which the city people call the "little village of songbirds." The Chanters themselves are fond of this nickname. Visitors to the little village enter through the Great Gate, which opens directly onto the Courtyard of Songs and its magical amphitheaters. Some visitors have cause to go through the Courtyard and up the broad steps to Marion Hall where they find their business in one of the offices or the library or perhaps the Assembly Room where the Chanters gather morning and night. The Courtyard of Songs and, to a lesser degree, Marion Hall, are the public venues of the little village. The rear entrance of Marion

Hall opens to the rest, the private part. Here are smaller courtyards, community gardens, many modest residences, and the slightly larger residences of the Head of the Cantori Branch and his Apprentices. Within the grounds they have a granary, a mill, a poultry shed, and a small pottery house. A few minor gates along the side and rear of the compound lead to the city or to the mountain road or to the Realm of the Phoenix.

Only a few people remain in the Courtyard of Songs. Nashua is tempted to hurry them along, but she stays in position, waiting with everyone else.

Apprentice Terridon comes down the front steps of Marion Hall and stands still. He meets her eyes, but instead of giving her the usual playful expression, he is sober. She gives him a questioning look. He shakes his head, *Not now*, and fixes his attention on the Courtyard. He is waiting for their guests to leave as well, but for a different reason.

Something is wrong.

The line of Chanters meanders out of the long building and curls around the circular courtyard, which buzzes with the speculative whispers of those waiting. Inside, Sage Mylas is rumored to be lying on his bed, sick and nearly dying. The Phoenix is bringing its egg of ash tonight. As Head of one of the seven branches of the Order, Sage Mylas must be at the Rock of Light to collect their share of ash for their branch. He should already be on his way. "Who will bring the ash?" a young Chanter nearby whispers. *Apprentice Terridon,* Nashua thinks. Someone nearby offers this same theory. Apprentice Terridon is a worthy candidate, but it should be Sage Mylas' privilege. They are silent with the unfairness of it all.

From the front of the line a solitary voice begins to sing; the rest join in. Without fresh ash for their horns there is no magic in the song to carry it to the hearts and minds of the listeners, but it matters not. Music has a power all its own. The Chanters sing the Miller's Ballad, which tells of the Miller's daughter lying sick in her bed. Her mother nurses the delicate child as the father stands helplessly by, singing his daughter a song in hopes that it will heal her. The Miller's Ballad ends without saying whether or not the child lives. It is a song for the sick. A beacon of hope for those who go on to get well. A tender farewell for those who slip to the other side.

Nashua's throat tightens; her companions finish the song without her.

Lindall comes out of the building and his sober expression quiets the crowd. Nashua reaches toward him but stays in her place when he notices and joins her. Her husband is the first of the higher-ranking members she has seen since Apprentice Terridon first summoned them to Sage Mylas' residence. Nashua is not the only one eager to hear news and several people form a circle around them.

Lindall looks at Nashua and takes a deep breath.

"Is he truly sick?" she asks.

Lindall nods. "Very, but he may yet recover. He is fighting. I think we can hope."

She wants to hope but worries anyway. "Is he saying his goodbyes? Does he think it his time?"

"No. He is picking his delegate to the Rock of Light."

Their little audience gasps.

"Apprentice Terridon," Nashua says.

"It seems not to be."

"It must be," she insists.

"I am fairly certain it is not," and his tone is the firm tone of her husband. Nashua answers with silence but a young Chanter speaks up.

"Who else?"

"Not I," Lindall replies. "Whatever I said, it was not what he was looking for." Several people press him for more information at once and he stills them with his hand. "He will ask you a question and you will give your answer."

"What is the question?" Nashua asks.

"I suspect it is different for each of us," Lindall says.

This gets the little circle pondering and he walks on.

Nashua's Choice

Nashua first met Sage Mylas six years ago during an interview to see if she would be allowed to join this magical society of Chanters. Only a few weeks before, Lindall, in his travels for the branch, had come across Nashua singing in the woods near her family's mountain home. Her song caught his attention and he immediately considered her as a possible recruit. But it was more than that. In spite of her youth—11 years his junior—and her bare feet and wild hair, not to mention the peculiarity of her eyes, Lindall found her enchanting. Nashua, young and inexperienced, found his enchantment enchanting. Who had ever seen so much in her?

Soon after, in a flush of love bright and brief as an early Spring flower, she returned to the little village as Lindall's bride and the newest person seeking initiation. Lindall had carefully selected a song he felt would best accentuate her voice; she had practiced it diligently on the road between her mountain home and the little village. How badly she wanted this new life, but what if Sage Mylas sent her away? How could she disappoint her new husband so soon?

She remembers that meeting in Sage Mylas' office, the window behind him open to the private side of the little village, the smell of fresh oranges from a bowl of blossoms on the desk. She expected to simply sing and hear his judgment, but no. He wanted to talk. She fingered the rough hem of her bodice coverlet, worrying the fabric into a wrinkled ball as she answered first one question, then another. Eventually his ease and warm smile overcame her and her hands stilled. She told him more than she meant to. She even confessed her embarrassment about her eyes. Her wish that she didn't have such an abnormality.

He looked softly surprised and examined her freely. A familiar feeling of naked exposure took her. She is unable to hide this strangeness about herself, her one eye blue and the other brown. So often she looks away from strangers to avoid seeing them look away from her. Sage Mylas held her gaze, however, and she let him see her shame.

"Ah, young Nashua. Others do not need to belittle you. You do it to yourself."

His words caused her to sit back in her seat, but he was not cruel. Neither did he weaken his message with timidness.

"Do you not know we are all unique and strange? This is one of life's great beauties. There is not one kind of flower, but hundreds of them. There is not one kind of songbird, but many, each unique. How gray the world would be with nothing but poppies and mockingbirds. Can one person be replaced with another? It cannot be done, for that person is unique and there is no other like him. This is as it should be.

Let your eyes remind you that you are a flower of a different sort, a bird like no other. Sing and be glad you can give the world your own kind of song. Think of your beautiful eyes, young Nashua, and be proud."

Nashua wondered if there were magic even in his speech, for something extraordinary had happened. His words filled her with peace, love, and acceptance. She felt warm and safe and joyful. At last, he asked her to sing for him. She abandoned the song she had originally planned, and sang instead a simple folk tale. It was a song about a young girl and her brother, about how he takes her picking flowers and shows her the rabbit's hiding place and carries her basket all the way home. She didn't know why that particular song came into her head. She simply wanted him to hear it and be wrapped in the feelings she felt when she sang it. Her song was an embrace.

When she finished, he smiled and told her she would first be assigned to sing the Song of Comfort. "You haven't much to learn, my dear."

The line advances and Nashua steps into the shelter of the building at last. Sage Mylas' apartment is surprisingly modest. A small living area holds two couches, a writing desk, and several bookcases loaded with manuscripts and folios. An adobe fireplace, cold and dark this time of year, sits in one corner. She has never come to this private place before. She has only ever visited with Sage Mylas in his office or seen him in Marion Hall or on the grounds. In spite of the many tender conversations they have had over the years, Nashua realizes she does not know him as well as she thinks she does. *He has lived a whole other life I know nothing about.* There is a small stuffed owl on a shelf, a worn quilt on the back of one couch, an alabaster box on the mantle. The entire room is filled with his presence and his absence all at once.

Once in Sage Mylas' private chamber, Nashua sees her master lying on his bed. How diminished he appears. His skin lacks its usual color, his eyes their vigor. Is he truly dying? The honey incense burning by his bed mingles with the ripe smell of sickness. On the other side of the bed, a man and a woman sit in somber attendance. Surrounded by bottles and bowls and the instruments of the sick, Nashua takes these individuals to be the physician and nurse. She looks toward the rear door where Apprentice Terridon stands watch. He meets her eyes and gives her a knowing glance. She realizes she has been staring openly and composes herself so that Sage Mylas will see no reflection of his poor health on her face.

Sage Mylas gestures the next person forward, a young Chanter who is only in his first year at the little village. Sage Mylas speaks so softly that the Chanter must lean forward so Sage Mylas can speak directly into his ear. Sage Mylas listens as the young man whispers his reply. In a voice that is almost the voice Nashua knows, Sage Mylas says "Very good," pats the back of the youthful hand resting on his covers, and sends him on his way. The young man exits through an adjoining room and out the door to the rear. Sage Mylas looks to the next in line and beckons with a mere smile, like a mother drawing a favored child into her arms.

How often Nashua has been the recipient of this same loving care. She frequently marvels at Sage Mylas' ability, in spite of his pressing responsibilities, to talk to each member of his little flock of songbirds as if he has nothing else in this world to do. When Nashua first arrived here, a little country girl hoping to find her place, she fairly glowed under Sage Mylas' love and attention. She believed she must be something dear to him for him to give her such fatherly care. When she opened her eyes enough to notice him treating everyone just the same, she initially felt disappointment that she was not the only one. This feeling was quenched by her admiration for such a man with such a heart. Her love for him only grew and she came to depend upon his tender counsel.

How would she get along without him?

Only three members stand between Nashua and Sage Mylas. He breaks into hacking coughs that make Nashua's own chest hurt. They all stand in mute impotence as the doctor and nurse efficiently provide a washrag, into which Sage Mylas coughs up some mucus. Nashua looks to Apprentice Terridon in appeal. They should not be audience to this. They should spare Sage Mylas his dignity.

The coughing subsides and Sage Mylas is given water. He settles on his cushions, his breathing labored. The doctor and nurse again take their seats. They wait in silence as Sage Mylas' breathing softens and he raises a hand to summon the next person. As with all the others, he whispers something to his listener and considers the reply. He concludes each brief conference with a "Very good" and a pat on the hand.

Nashua looks to Apprentice Terridon standing guard. She looks down the line, dwindling fast, and sees no one suitable to go as Sage Mylas' proxy. She considers Apprentice Terridon again, and he meets her eye. She sees her sorrow reflected in his eyes. Sage Mylas must truly be dying. Perhaps this is his way of saying goodbye without causing his little flock too much grief. Maybe all he really wants is to look into each pair of eyes, pat each hand, and say "Very good."

After so long a wait, the moment comes to Nashua suddenly and she is the one Sage Mylas gazes upon, the one drawing near to him, the one kneeling by his bedside. She is completely taken in by the presence of this great man, so pale and weak and lovely. It is just as it was when she first met him. If they were alone, she would sing to him again. She would sing him the song of the brother and sister and wrap him up in it. But they are not alone, and she bends toward him, as she saw the others do, so he can whisper in her ear. Her shoulder presses against his arm, surprisingly soft with age. Here, she thinks, is a man, not merely a Sage. He is facing his death. With all these many about, who is here to comfort him? She places her hand on his, as a mother would her child, a gesture concealed from the others as she leans close to him. It is all the comfort she can give.

His shallow breathing sounds in her ear. She waits for her Sage to speak, but he says nothing.

She rocks back slightly and looks him in the eyes. He looks back with a strange expression and she is afraid. Sage Mylas grasps her hand with fierceness. *Oh heaven, don't let him die now.* Still no speech. She does not know if he is trying to speak or if another coughing fit looms. *Water,* she thinks, and glances at the physician for help. The physician takes no notice but he cannot see this look on the face of her Sage and he cannot feel the way Sage Mylas grips her hand.

"Sage Mylas," she whispers, determined to nurse the man herself, "may I fetch you something?"

In a trembling voice that is, nevertheless, loud enough for all in the room to hear, Sage Mylas replies, "Fetch me the ash."

Two

It is all a confusing blur. Apprentice Terridon takes Nashua round the shoulders and whispers in her ear, "We must hurry." They do not exit the room out the rear as others have done, but rather follow the line back out the front door, down the steps, and through the courtyards. Apprentice Terridon has one arm around her, hand on her shoulder, his other hand on the shoulder nestled close to him. He escorts her through the grounds like an invalid. Indeed, she feels light in the head and spongy on her feet and it is not until they are approaching a carriage at the Great Gate that she thinks to look about for her husband. Lindall is nowhere to be seen. Several people have followed this scene and gathered round. She realizes they are talking, all at once it seems. She hears Apprentice Terridon declare her bearer of the ash. They enter the carriage and she spies Lindall at last. He lingers on the edge of the crowd, far from her. A conversation passes between them in the brief moment that their eyes meet before the carriage lurches forward and away. Her unease intensifies as she thinks of Lindall's face. Nashua notices the sun is well into its descent; soon it will begin its colorful theatrics to mark the end of another day. This startles her still further. Where did the day go? Apprentice Terridon is talking, talking, talking. Nashua watches him and realizes he is giving her instructions. She tries to listen but it is all noise. Her mind cannot sort it out.

"A moment!" she says, and he stops with his mouth agape. "Please."

He sits back and offers her the requested reprieve. Her mind drinks in the silence. A few moments pass and she begins to absorb what is happening. She is going to the Rock of Light. She will be the one to fetch the ash instead of Sage Mylas. *Sage Mylas.* She didn't even say goodbye.

She is going to the Rock of Light. How did this happen?

Houses, shops, and people pass before her view as the carriage brings them ever nearer to their destination. She can smell the salty sea air. They are getting close.

She is going to the Rock of Light and has no idea what she is to do once she gets there. Fetch the ash? How?

Nashua's Choice

She looks to Apprentice Terridon and pleads, "Tell me what to do," as if he hadn't been trying to do that already.

He gives her his open, boyish smile. It is a comfort to see such normalcy after such a day. "You will only need to remember a few things, but you must remember them exactly. Nothing may deviate from the ceremony. That is the first thing. You must follow the ceremony in every way."

Nashua nods.

"You may not even turn your head when you're not supposed to."

"Yes."

"Almost always you will follow Sage Inne." Sage Inne is Head of the Eala Branch, as well as Head of the entire Order. Nashua has seen her and heard her speak in Assembly, but she has never interacted with her directly. "Only once will you do something different, and that is to sing. You can do that. Everything else is to follow the others. Oh, and there is one bit of magic, but it is not hard. Early magic. One of the first given. Every branch can do this bit, so it is not hard."

Nashua wants to believe it is not hard but she is nervous anyway. She listens as Apprentice Terridon goes through the ceremony and describes the magic she is to perform, for the first time, when they are right in the middle of the ceremony. The magic is to return a small portion of the ash. She cannot practice it now because the orb is at the Rock of Light and they are in this jolting carriage speeding on their way. Apprentice Terridon has her practice saying the spell and assures her it will work. She knows him well enough to sense his anxiety on her behalf. "Some of the first magic the Phoenix taught us," he says again. "It is easy because no one does it but once and that is only every several hundred years for this one ceremony."

She nods.

"When the flame regenerates, that is when you sing the Song of Calling." He glances at her pewter horn necklace. "You know this song." She nods. She does indeed. Every Chanter learns the five Songs of the Phoenix, even though most of them never get to sing them when it is time. Five songs, sung just one time each over the course of the lifetime of the Phoenix. Hundreds of years. Hundreds of thousands of Chanters practicing all that time. Only five get to sing them in all their power. Nashua would be one of them.

She feels her chest lift and lighten with excitement. She will get to sing the Song of Calling. As she ponders this imminent event, Apprentice Terridon continues with his instructions, detailing the ceremony, emphasizing again that she must maintain complete formality and reverence.

"You must not deviate from the ceremony at all."

"Yes, I know."

"Not even to turn your head. Not even to look for it. Sage Inne will watch for the Phoenix. When she sees it approaching, she will lead you all into position. Then it will bring the egg of ash."

Apprentice Terridon stops. The wheels of the carriage are on cobblestone now and the noise fills the carriage. Nashua is struck again with the strangeness of this situation. Why is she so privileged to do this? Why was she chosen to see the Phoenix when she is not even an Apprentice?

"I'm sorry Terridon. It should have been you."

"It should have been Sage Mylas."

"Yes, of course. But if not him... you. I'm sorry. I wasn't trying to make this happen."

Apprentice Terridon leans in and takes her hands. Her heart pounds. "I had no thought of this myself. I thought it would be Sage Mylas, like you." He shrugs. He is not holding it against her. "Maybe you will be an Apprentice now. It doesn't matter. Do you know what I would do if I were in your shoes?"

She shakes her head.

"I would *revel* in it."

He pats her knees and laughs, that old familiar laugh she loves so. They could be on their way to a picnic, he is so lighthearted. He reaches down to a trunk to one side of their feet. "If I were you," he says as he pulls out a long, black cloak, "I would hold on to every moment with a glad heart." He wraps the cloak around her and helps her put her arms in the wide sleeves. "I would think to myself, *I get to see the Phoenix. I'm going to remember everything.*"

He arranges the material at her shoulders so it all hangs correctly and she stands slightly to smooth the fabric beneath her before sitting down again.

"I would not," he says looking at her directly, "allow guilt or wondering to ruin such a momentous occasion."

Nashua feels his words lightening her heart as he brings a small cedar box out of the trunk and sets it on her lap. He opens the lid to reveal a pile of ash, the size of a small anthill. It is all they have left from the Phoenix's last regeneration over 800 years ago. When she leaves the Rock of Light tonight, she will bring back the box full of ash. It is the source of all their magic. The heart of everything they do. Her grip on the box tightens and she has a sudden fear of coming out of the Rock of Light, tripping, and spilling the new ash all over the ground.

"What if I do something wrong?"

"Your job is to sing for our beloved Phoenix. You can do that, can't you?"

She smiles.

"That's my girl. Sage Inne will divide the ash among the seven branches. All you have to do is bring ours home."

"But do not deviate from the ceremony," she says, teasing.

"Oh no," he says, his face serious again. "Don't do that."

Nashua's Choice

🕯🕯🕯 🕯🕯🕯 🕯🕯🕯

The Rock of Light sits at the end of a weather-beaten outcropping reaching into the sea. It is an ancient structure, shaped like a lighthouse with rough openings all around the upper section. No one knows for certain just when it was built, only that the Phoenix created it, far from the Realm in which the Phoenix lives its many lives for its own mysterious purposes. The purpose of the Rock of Light, however, is clear. In the center of the upper room, the Eternal Flame burns. Its light shines through the great openings of the upper section. It burns brightly at the beginning of the Phoenix's life, dimly as time wears on. The Eternal Flame reflects the life cycle of the Phoenix. The Chanters stand guard morning and night, watching for certain changes in the Flame and announcing those changes with the Songs of the Phoenix. It is how they know when the Phoenix is going to regenerate. It is how the seven branches of the Order know to gather for the ash.

Seven branches, the Cantori Branch and its Chanters being one, all use the ash as the source of their magic. The Murano Branch makes their great glass objects that are infused with magical qualities. The Eala Branch is for the women who transform into great golden birds. The Layrin Branch, who Nashua considers closest to her branch since they are such thoughtful mystics like the Chanters, have wonderful ways with their enchanted vines and shrubbery. The Wysard Branch, with their spell-casting witches and wizards, are the most powerful and diverse group. The Dianese Branch is a mystery to all.

The branches use their magic to benefit one another—the Layrin Branch tends the enchanted vines in the Chanters' many auditoriums—but branches do not share their magical secrets. They have each been taught their secrets by the Phoenix, and developed many more on their own. The Phoenix ash is at the heart of it all.

When the Phoenix dies, it bursts into flame and is wholly consumed until nothing remains but ash. It rises from the ash, more glorious than ever, and rolls its ash into an egg. It brings its gift to the Rock of Light where the seven Heads wait. Or, in this case, the Heads and Nashua.

The carriage stops near the base of the Rock of Light. The sky and sea are alight with the setting sun: an entire vista of oranges, yellows, and reds blazing on the clouds and winking on the waters. Apprentice Terridon helps her out of the carriage and escorts her into the little room at the base of the Rock of Light where the Head of the Order waits.

"Sage Inne," Apprentice Terridon says, inclining his head. "May I present Nashua of Landsdowne, Chanter of the Cantori Branch. She is Sage Mylas' chosen proxy."

Nashua's Choice

Sage Inne is a tall woman with cropped gray hair, a hooked nose, and a long neck. This is as close as Nashua has ever been to her and finds her presence even more impressive than normal. Sage Inne steps forward inspecting Nashua, who bows her head in respect. "Are you an Apprentice?" Sage Inne asks.

Nashua shakes her head and Apprentice Terridon answers, "No."

There is a pause as Sage Inne's face expresses, then represses, her surprise. "Well then, so be it. There is no time for wondering."

"I have given her the instructions."

"Thank you," Sage Inne says and turns toward the inner door that leads to the stairs, gesturing for Nashua to follow.

"I will be waiting for you," Apprentice Terridon says. "Just outside."

Nashua's throat constricts as fresh nerves fill her; she merely nods. Apprentice Terridon gives her a big grin and she smiles in reply. They pass through the door and close it tightly. Sage Inne gives her own instructions about the ceremony as they ascend the spiraling staircase that leads to the top of the Rock of Light. Though Nashua has made this climb countless times to take her turn standing watch over the Phoenix's flame, the climb seems longer this time. More awkward too, as she must concentrate to keep her balance while carrying the box and lifting the hem of Sage Mylas' cloak, which is a bit too long for her.

Nashua's Choice

She listens carefully to the ceremony procedures. They are familiar enough by this time since Apprentice Terridon went over them twice and had her repeat them back to him a third. Apprentice Terridon seems to have done a thorough job with the instructions; Sage Inne does not add anything new.

At the top of the stairs they emerge into the upper room. Familiar though this room is, it seems different to her now. Normally she would be here with only two other Chanters. Now there are six other people in the room, all wearing the same cloak to indicate their coveted status as members of the Order. There is a hushed bustling as they come to greet her, to subtly (or not so subtly) inspect her, and move into position. Nashua places her box next to six others on a long, low shelf against the door. There is a single glass orb sitting on the shelf. Into this she places a pinch of ash from their box, joins her companions at the altar, and sets the orb on the tablet in front of her. Seven orbs in place. They are ready.

The sun has dipped below the horizon and the colors drain from the sky. The Phoenix's flame is very slight indeed. They have only a small wait yet. Nashua's nerves and excitement bump around inside her. She is not used to being so agitated in front of the Phoenix's flame. It seems contrary to how things ought to be. While the citizens of the city and the local villages come to the Chanters in their auditoriums for comfort or healing or strength, the Chanters come to the Rock of Light. They guard the Eternal Flame, yes, but their watches become a kind of meditation. A consolation. A source of peace and strength.

Nashua wonders what these other members of the Order think of the Phoenix's flame. Only the Chanters stand guard. Do the other branches love the flame as she does? What are they thinking, standing in this silent circle, as they gaze upon its soft, clear light? Do they feel the connection to the Phoenix as well? Or perhaps they don't need it in the same way. Apprentices and Heads are permitted to make periodic journeys into the Realm itself, to study the Phoenix and who knows what else. The Phoenix is such a strange and marvelous creature. Every few thousand years it teaches the Order something new. Nashua knows not how, given the Phoenix is a creature, not a man, and does not talk like a man. But how does the Phoenix do anything that it does? How did it create the Rock of Light? How did it first begin the Order? How does it pull itself out of death's grip to live again? The chosen few who journey to the Realm in the name of studying it do not seem to come back with new knowledge or new magic. Perhaps all they do is go and watch in wonder.

Nashua may not ever journey to the Realm. She may not ever be an Apprentice—she does not give weight to Terridon's passing explanation to the strange events of the day—but this night she will see the Phoenix with her own eyes. As she watches its flame, waiting for the sign that the Phoenix has extinguished its life, she settles at last into the familiar comfort of being in this place and feeling its power. More so than usual, she is glowing inside, just as the Eternal Flame glows before her. If she doubted earlier, she feels certain now: the Phoenix accepts her presence here.

The Eternal Flame shudders, collapses to a wisp, and flickers out. Just like that. After burning for the last 1074 years, the Eternal Flame is gone. Nashua senses a communal shudder at such a strange and lonely sight. The chill night air creeps in through the open windows, past the circle of cloaked figures, and into the void left by the flame.

They each hold their glass orb. Nashua's palms are sweaty and she longs to dry them. As if reading her mind, Sage Inne casts her a warning glance. Nashua does not need it. She is motionless, waiting her turn.

The man opposite Nashua, his cloak a ghost of color in the near darkness, raises his orb over the coals on the altar. He rotates it until the opening in the top faces downward. "Relessa." The puff of ash falls from his orb and settles on the coals. She watches this bit of magic and reminds herself that he has never performed the spell either. Surely it will work for her as it worked for him? He turns his orb upright and places it on the stone tablet in front of him. Around the circle the releasing ceremony progresses, through two more Order members until it comes, all so abruptly, to Nashua. She raises the orb, walking her fingers along its surface, rotating it, praising her steady hands. "*Relessa*," she says. In spite of Apprentice Terridon's assurances, in spite of witnessing the successful performance of this spell by those before her, she is astonished to see the ash obey her command. She glances at the interior of the orb as she sets it on the tablet in front of her. Not a hint of ash remains. She has returned each speck to the Phoenix's altar, exactly as instructed.

The ceremony continues around the circle, ending with Sage Inne returning her Branch's ash. Sage Inne raises her hands, the sleeves of her cloak sliding down her arms, and speaks with the rhythm of a drum: "*Eta retune. Eta retune. Eta retune.*" She lowers her arms. They are but minutes away.

All are silent. Except for the last light of day, all is dark.

The coals burst into life, flames roaring toward them so that Nashua and her companions cannot resist flinching away. The Eternal Flame halts, illuminating the cloaked members of the Order and the entire upper room of the Rock of Light. They regain their composure and settle back into position, though Nashua wishes they were a few steps back. This is not the minute flame she has known; its heat is overwhelming. She can see now why the altar of coals is so large. The Eternal Flame dances boldly in all its glory.

Sage Inne meets her eyes as all awareness in the room turns to Nashua. She is the Chanter who will announce this change of the Eternal Flame to every ear in the land. Suppressing her nerves, she focuses on her task. The pewter horn around her neck warms and vibrates at the first note of the Song of Calling. She is no longer aware of the Rock of Light, the Order members, the ceremony. All she sees is the Eternal Flame in front of her. All she feels is the magical power of this vast song, beginning within her and reaching across the land to every soul in it. She is immersed in power, her body pulsing with the pewter horn. The last note leaves her, the song fades away, and the magic goes with it. She is only Nashua again, standing in the middle of the Rock of Light. In the silence that follows, she is surprised at her mournful longing for the Song. She will never sing with such intensity again.

It is time to move. Sage Inne leads the group around the altar to their final position facing the Pillar. They are a more comfortable distance from the Eternal Flame, which casts its heat as it blazes behind them. Raised in front of them, the cup-shaped Pillar of Receiving waits. Beyond the Pillar is the window facing in the direction of the Realm of the Phoenix, and now, at last, Nashua can look for herself.

Nashua's Choice

A veil of darkness sweeps over the land, approaching them, concealing what she so longs to see. It rushes forward until it completely surrounds the Rock of Light in darkness. Nashua knows the Great Darkness is everywhere. The only light anywhere in the land is inside this tower, coming from the Eternal Flame behind them, brought to life when the Phoenix resurrected itself in the Realm.

Now, after its journey from the Realm to the Rock of Light, cloaked in darkness along the way, the Phoenix emerges before them.

The Glorious Bird.

Nashua now knows why the Phoenix is so called. Its feathers are so brilliant they appear still to be aflame. Its eyes shine and dance as if made of glowing embers. She wants to bow before its beauty and can scarcely bear to look at it. The Phoenix is so large it fills the window, dwarfing the members standing weak-kneed in front of it. The wind from its wings beat back her hair and cloak. She feels nearly as much heat from the Phoenix as from its flame behind her.

The Phoenix hovers over the pillar between it and the Order members. In its claws is a massive egg of ash. With elegance, the Phoenix sets the egg on the pillar. Sage Inne bows and they follow her lead. Nashua hears the Phoenix flying away and she suppresses the urge to cry out, *Don't go!* They straighten and the Phoenix is already in the distance, the darkness retreating with it, leaving only the first moonlight in its wake. Nashua's skin tingles from the spectacle she has just witnessed.

The egg of ash draws her attention. It is glowing. The tingling in her skin becomes unpleasant. *Is this supposed to happen?* She sneaks a glance at Sage Inne, who has begun her ceremonial approach toward the pillar. She is erect and stately as ever, but looks like someone trying not to appear alarmed.

Nashua looks back to see a ball of light emerging from the egg, expanding past it. She forces her feet to stay in position as the ball of light grows larger and larger and nearer to where they all stand. She cannot help it. She looks at the other members for guidance. Decorum is fading. They are each appealing to Sage Inne for help. *This is not supposed to happen.*

Sage Inne signals for them to stay in their places but she has halted herself. The ball of light is growing. Nashua wants to run forward and pull Sage Inne away as the light draws ever nearer. She is rooted to the ground. She watches transfixed as the light touches Sage Inne who cries out in pain and leaps backward. They all flinch in response. Nashua looks to the egg of ash, the center of this growing ball of light.

She could not look away now even if she wanted to. The ball of light presses toward them. All down the line Order members jerk away as if burned. Nashua feels no pain as the light presses on her. She is bound in place by delicious warmth as the light passes through her. All around her, the ball of light is a pulsating dome of color. She is inside of it, alone.

She feels a strange sensation, one she has never felt before. It seems to come from within her, yet from without at the same time. It is both a prompting and a thought. The thought is this: *retrieve the egg.*

She dares not. Only Sage Inne may retrieve the egg.

The light brightens, as if in response to her mental resistance. As if urging her on. The light is nearly blinding and she squints against it, but she cannot take her eyes off the egg. Maybe she should not obey, but she can no longer resist. She moves forward, approaching the pillar. She climbs the steps, the egg of ash its own powerful presence before her.

She hesitates.

What consequences will this bring? Again, the prompting to act. What can she do? She reaches up, cups the egg in both hands, and brings it down. She holds it somewhat awkwardly; it is heavier than she imagined. It has a slightly rough texture, like that of porous stone.

The surface cracks, splinters, and suddenly the entire thing is crumbling. Nashua's heart leaps into her throat as she fumbles to contain the ash and what is inside. She drops to her knees in an effort to salvage it. The egg of ash is more than just ash. In fact, there is hardly any ash at all and what little there is, she realizes with horror, is strewn on her gown and the floor around her. Shining in her hands are three stones.

They are almost as long as her hand but not nearly as wide, and come to a soft point at each end. They are of different colors but equally luminous. Three stones—red, blue, and yellow—calling to her so strongly she thinks her heart may fail her.

Before she can think what this might mean, Nashua starts speaking. These are not her words. It isn't her voice. It is low, melodious, sorrowful, powerful. It is the Phoenix speaking to her, speaking through her. The words pass out of her mouth and they are imprinted into her mind. She speaks them, but it is as if she is listening to someone speaking to her.

She can hardly bear the message.

The message ends. Silence falls. The ball of light withdraws and vanishes. Nashua rocks on the floor, clutches the stones to her chest, and shivers in the chill that penetrates this room full of light.

Three

"Let me see," Sage Inne says.

Still on the floor, Nashua did not notice Sage Inne's approach. Nashua does not move.

"Nashua. Let me see."

Nashua opens her quaking hands but keeps the stones close. Their beauty alone is enough to make one stare. The others tentatively gather round.

Nashua watches Sage Inne kneel and stare at the stones, fiercely luminous. Sage Inne reaches out her hand. In the space that exists between the stones and the waiting hand of Sage Inne, Nashua senses a trembling warning.

She gathers the stones closer to her body, enclosing them in her embrace. A collective gasp escapes the group, excepting Sage Inne who remains still as stone and a man who cries "Insolence!"

It happens in an instant.

Nashua's Choice

He steps forward, his intent to deliver the stones to Sage Inne himself clear. Nashua flinches away and Sage Inne raises her hand in warning, bringing the man to a halt.

Only an instant, but Nashua's heart flails against her chest. He may as well have been after her head.

"No," Sage Inne says without removing her eyes from Nashua. "No. The Phoenix has made its choice clear." Sage Inne lowers her hand. Nashua wonders if she felt the vibrating warning as well. It makes no matter. Nashua guards the stones as if protecting her own child. She cannot fathom it, but she will die before letting anyone in this room remove these stones from her grasp.

No one moves. Her pulse slowly returns to normal as nobody else seems inclined to force the issue.

"The ash," someone whispers.

For the first time since the Phoenix's departure, Nashua speaks in her own voice. "The ash you can have."

Nashua has managed to stand and gather round the Eternal Flame with the others. Sage Inne is circling the group, magically dividing the ash into seven parts and depositing it into the glass orbs. Nashua does not know how she will perform the rest of the ceremony properly, for she refuses to let the stones out of her grasp. She would not even want to deposit them into a pocket, if the cloak had pockets. She could manage to retrieve the orb with one hand if she balanced it against the top of her hip bone, like carrying a baby. Even if the ceremony allowed for such unorthodox behavior, what then?

Sage Inne returns to her place in the circle. The ash, what little there was, is divided among the branches. Sage Inne glances uncomfortably at Nashua, then glances at Nashua's chest. Sage Inne does not even try to hide her astonishment. Nashua looks down. Stunned, she grabs the pewter horn at the end of her necklace and lifts it closer. Closer still. Embedded in the horn are three small red stones—stones that were not there prior to the Phoenix's visit.

Her head swims. She drops the horn and looks away. She cannot fathom what this means. She wishes she did not see it. What more? It is too much. She needs Sage Mylas. He sent her here. Surely he must know what to do. She remembers the strange promptings that led her to remove the egg of ash from its pillar. She thinks of the way the Phoenix talked to her and through her. What did Sage Mylas feel when he chose her? What did he know? She can't stay here any longer as if nothing has happened.

Nashua's patience with the ceremony flees. She no longer cares about what step to take when and when to lift her arms and when to stay still. Does the Phoenix even care? Let it strike her down if it does. She steps close to the tablet and, as if picking up a child, scoots the orb into her one free arm to the general outcry of the members.

"Enough," she says. It is all she can say. All her energy is required just to get where she needs to go.

No unnatural force strikes her to the ground and no human arm tries to stop her. She retreats to her box and here she has no choice but to set the stones on the table. With two shaking hands she deposits the ash in her box, bundles the stones in the excess fabric of her cloak, lifts the box under one arm, and leaves the upper room. She is so lightheaded she fears the journey down the long, long staircase. One arm cradles the box; the other protects the stones. As she descends she leans her shoulder against the stone wall for balance, eyes on the next step, and the next, and the next.

She reaches the bottom at last, crosses the anteroom, and exits the Rock of Light. Torches burn along the road to the city. There are people moving about and voices everywhere but it is all a scene of confusion and disorder to Nashua. She spots Apprentice Terridon, whose smile of triumph wilts the moment he sees her face.

"What is wrong?"

"Into the carriage."

He says a word to the driver; they enter promptly, and are off. Their departure from the Rock of Light is as hurried and disorienting as their arrival had been.

Unlike before, Apprentice Terridon is a model of silence, though his expression communicates enough. He fears to know what happened but she cannot talk. Beyond that, should she? She sees Apprentice Terridon eyeing the bundle of fabric concealing the stones. She presses the stones so firmly against her side her ribs smart with pain, yet she cannot lessen her grip. She cannot tell him about the stones. She cannot say a word. She must see Sage Mylas. He must know what to do. He will tell her what to do.

Apprentice Terridon's eyes light upon her necklace and his face slackens in surprise. She presses against the back of her seat.

"What on earth?" he says.

"No."

"What happened?"

"I need to see Sage Mylas."

He says no more but continues to gape at her. She looks out the window. The ride back feels impossibly long. There are lights and people and noises in the streets. Are they celebrating? Do they know? All they would have seen is the Great Darkness and, after its retreat, the revitalized Eternal Flame. No one could know. Apprentice Terridon doesn't know. Nashua feels alone in the little carriage. She would leap out and run to Sage Mylas if she thought it could get her there any faster.

As they approach the Great Gate, she sees a crowd of eager Chanters. They seem so exuberant. Perhaps they are expecting her triumphant exit from the carriage, holding the box aloft for all to see. Perhaps they are waiting to cheer her. Perhaps they would escort her all the way back to Sage Mylas. Perhaps that's all it is but the only thing Nashua can see is that her way is blocked.

"Go around," she says.

"What?"

"Meadowlark Gate. We'll enter that way. It's closest."

"Nashua what on earth is going on?"

The carriage begins to slow and her heart flails again. "Tell him!"

"Continue on," Apprentice Terridon hollers to the driver. "Hurry!" The carriage jolts and they pass the crowd, Nashua sinking away from the window. She does not look for her husband. When they are safely past, Apprentice Terridon calls, "Meadowlark Gate. Quickly."

"Thank you," she says.

He sits back as they round the outer boundaries of the little village and head for the side gate. He examines Nashua. She says nothing.

They stop at last. Apprentice Terridon exits first and extends his hand to her elbow to help her down. He is on the side with the stones. She freezes, looking at his outstretched palm. They linger there a moment. He glances at the cloak where she is concealing the stones. Their eyes meet. He looks down, drops his arm, and circles to her other side. He extends his hand again. This time she accepts his help out of the carriage. He holds her elbow firmly as she navigates down the steps.

They enter the little village through the minor gate, into a small courtyard lined with gardens. And no people.

At this point, Nashua runs.

She bursts into Sage Mylas' living room to find a group of higher-ranking members waiting. Her husband is among them. They stand upon her arrival but she hurries to Sage Mylas' door. Lindall rushes forward and meets her at the door, his hand on the handle.

He opens his mouth to say something but she cuts him short. "I need to see Sage Mylas."

He pauses and she sees his frustration. She decides she will edge past him if necessary but he says, "Of course" and pushes open the door for her. She enters the room, relieved to see Sage Mylas at last. He is still lying in his bed, awake and waiting for her. The physician and nurse are still by his bed. She forgot about them.

She hears Lindall closing the door behind her but she turns round. "Wait."

He pauses, the door half open.

Sage Mylas is trying to sit up and the physician and nurse have risen to help him. They help lift his upper body and prop him with pillows. It is agonizing to watch him struggle so. He settles into position but suffers another coughing fit. They attend to him and Nashua looks back to her husband. He gives her a questioning look but what can she say?

The coughing subsides at last and the physician and nurse go to resume their places. "I need to see Sage Mylas alone," she says.

They stop and stare at her.

"Nashua," she hears Lindall say behind her. "Sage Mylas is very ill."

Sage Mylas seems to look her over at last. His illness has not dulled his keenness. His eyes take in the box under one arm, the cloak bundling something under the other, her necklace, her face.

"Child?" Sage Mylas' voice sounds so weak.

"Alone. Please."

The physician begins his protest but Sage Mylas raises a shaky hand. "Leave us."

The nurse looks to the physician, who seems disinclined to move. He looks at Nashua, then back at Sage Mylas, and relents. "I'll be just outside."

They exit the room and Nashua follows, wanting to seal them away herself. The nurse leaves, the physician after her. Lindall lingers just outside the door. As she pushes the door shut his eyes land upon her necklace and shock registers on his face.

Alone at last, she rushes to her Sage and sits on the edge of the bed. Weak or not, poor man, she needs him to be her Sage. She needs him to tell her what to do. She rests the box of ash on the bed between them, but keeps the stones close as she relates her story. His face grows grave. At one point he pulls the box onto his lap and opens it to see for himself how little ash is inside. She sees the horror on his face but continues her story, hastening to tell him everything. She reveals the stones but keeps them cradled safely in the fabric, close to her chest. She delivers the message of the Phoenix, word for word. As if he needed an interpretation of the Phoenix's words, she adds in her own, "The Phoenix is in trouble. Someone's going to try to destroy it and keep its magic for themselves. Sage Mylas, what do we do?"

He looks at her with that strange, wondering expression he wore before he asked her to retrieve the ash.

"What? Sage Mylas, what is the Phoenix telling you?"

"It chose you," Sage Mylas says, almost to himself.

"Yes, but why? Is the Phoenix talking to you? Please tell me, what do I do?"

"The ash," he says looking down at it. "So little."

She lays her free hand on top of the stones. They are slightly warm. Or does she imagine them to be so? He looks at them, his brows furrowed.

"Sage Mylas," she says. "Please. I cannot let them go. What am I to do with these?"

"Do not ask me!" he says, and shrinks into his pillow as if threatened by a saber.

Nashua stares and sits back in surprise. Sage Mylas himself seems taken aback by his own words. "I'm sorry," he says, rubbing his face. "I'm sorry, my dear."

He takes a shaky breath and settles himself. "Well," he says, with the voice of authority she knows. Her hope in him grows. "Well," he says again, weak now. Her hope vanishes.

What of all this?

He knows no more than she does.

It sinks into her at last. She knew it the moment the stones fell into her hands, the ash spilling off their shining surfaces. These stones are for her and her alone. Sage Mylas cannot help her.

No one can.

She is in this alone, keeper of the stones until the time comes to deliver them to the rightful bearers. And what of that? Who are these bearers? The Phoenix's message is not entirely clear to her, but she understands enough. These stones will go to three bearers. They are the ones who must protect the Phoenix, or at least try. Until then, the stones are hers to guard.

There is more she must ponder, but her head aches. She brings a hand to her forehead, rubbing the tension there.

"The ash," Sage Mylas says again.

"Yes." That, at least, is his puzzle to solve. "You will tell us what to do," she says, tapping the box and standing. "I must go now."

"Nashua," he says. She looks at him, so pale and thin. "I am sorry."

She takes a deep breath. Her dear Sage. How can she fault him?

"*In a wood full of poppies,*" Nashua sings, "*a poor lass passes by.*" Sage Mylas smiles faintly, recognizing the folk song she sang to him during their first meeting. Still singing, she turns away and opens the door.

Lindall is there and she allows herself to lean into his arms, the stones cradled on the side opposite him. The physician and nurse return to their patient, shutting the door as she sings, "*Her fair brother spies cottontail, bounding away.*"

Apprentice Terridon has joined the group waiting in Sage Mylas' living room. All eyes are upon her. She thinks of how this evening should have gone, with Sage Mylas presenting the ash in Marion Hall, the grand feast, the late-night lantern procession to the Rock of Light so everyone could see the Eternal Flame for themselves.

It was meant to be a joyous night.

Only she and Sage Mylas know just how wrong it went. She has no idea what those in the room expect to happen next. She has no idea what the rest of the branch expects to happen next. Whatever it is, whatever celebrations they may plan on continuing without Sage Mylas, they will have to carry on without her as well. Still leaning into her husband she says, "Take me home."

He escorts her firmly, his authority reasserted. She is content to let him lead her, to act as buffer between her and all who approach, to guide her safely home.

But what is safety? As they go out into the night and pass one little dwelling after another, the front gardens lit up by celebratory torches, Nashua feels something nagging at her bones. They come to their tiny cottage, halfway between Marion Hall and Sage Mylas' residence. They pass through their garden, through the front door, and into the familiar living room with its white-plastered walls glowing yellow from the fire in the hearth. She feels she is bringing the burden of the stones into her own home. Into her place of refuge. Among the people she loves most.

Lindall's mother sits at the dining table in the kitchen and releases the young child who is scrambling off her lap. Nashua drops to her knees and brings the toddling boy into a one-armed embrace. She nuzzles her face onto his shoulder as he wraps his little arms around his mother's neck.

Four

Three days after the Phoenix's regeneration, Nashua lies awake in bed. It is not yet dawn. The house is still and Lindall sleeps so quietly that Nashua periodically holds her own breath to confirm he is still breathing. She does not understand how he can sleep. How anyone can sleep. She cannot get more than a few hours at a time.

The last few days have been one series of blows after another. The rumors began the very night of the Phoenix's visit. The light of dawn confirmed things the next morning. She had only to climb the hill behind the granary to see for herself; away in the distance, sheer walls of smooth rock rose into the sky, all around the Realm of the Phoenix. It is as if the Phoenix lifted the entire Realm high into the air. They still await word from scouting parties sent out in both directions, one by sea, one by land. They will circumvent the

Realm and, likely, bring back reports of what she already knows. The Realm is cut off.

Nashua listened to talk of the mysterious bridge all day before she would allow Apprentice Terridon and Lindall to take her to see it for herself. Up the coast from the Rock of Light, nearer to the city, a stone bridge stretches out into the sea. Like the cliffs, the bridge had not been there before the Phoenix's visit. The stone bridge hovers above the water, unsupported by pillars of any sort, and hums with the hum of fresh and powerful magic. Boats have gone out far enough to see that it ends abruptly over the water, leading nowhere, but no one has dared set foot on it. Not yet. Apprentice Terridon suggested Nashua be the one to do it. She flatly refused, for the bridge scared her more than anything she'd yet seen. He tried to persuade her, pulling her away from Lindall to whisper, "You were chosen to receive the ash."

She replied, "I was chosen for the ash. Not for this." She retreated to Lindall, asking him to take her home.

After they left the bridge, Terridon stewing in his frustration with her and Lindall casting contemplative looks between his two companions, they returned to the little village only to learn of Sage Mylas' passing. The entire branch mourns for him, but Nashua feels apart from them all and alone in her grief. There is an ache in her chest, but tears do not come. She is too lost for any of it. Apprentice Terridon says she is the next

Head of their branch and feels certain the Order will agree. As far as he is concerned it is only a step away from being official except that Nashua will hear nothing of it. It is ludicrous. On the night of the Phoenix's return, Sage Mylas met with Apprentice Terridon and told him everything. Nashua feels Sage Mylas trusted Terridon with the secret of the stones and the prophecy, and by doing so, indicated who his successor should be. Terridon insists that was an act of mere delegation. He says the Phoenix chose her over him to receive the stones, chose her over the Head of the entire Order, so it is easy to see who should be Head of their branch. When Terridon addressed her as Sage to make his point, she grew hot and tight in the face and told him that if he ever addressed her as such again she would banish him from Villacita Cantori forever. A rash and ridiculous threat she could only carry out if she were, in fact, Head of the branch, but it had the desired effect. He has not pressed the matter since. Still, it has only been a couple of days and she senses he is giving her space, not conceding. It matters not.

She has overheard conversations between Apprentice Terridon, Lindall, and Lindall's mother Phaedra. Lindall questions whether Nashua should be the next Head. Who wouldn't? She is not even an Apprentice. Who in the branch would follow her aside from Terridon? Lindall and his mother have asked Apprentice Terridon many questions about what happened at the Rock of Light, the meaning of the stones in her necklace, and what she's hiding. Terridon, to his credit, gives nothing away. He only tells them to be patient with her, to support her. A foreign concept perhaps. Lindall has not spoken to her about it at all. Though pensive and clearly curious, Lindall only speaks to her about small things: that he'll be at Marion Hall for the afternoon or to encourage her to eat or to tell her to rest. Sleep eludes her. Lindall believes this is because so much has happened at once, because she must be overwhelmed by it all. Perhaps.

The truth is Nashua thinks on all the events of the past three days with numbness, as if she is in a glass box watching them unfold from neutral territory. The truth is, she cannot relax for fear of the stones. She took them with her, in a waist pouch satchel hidden under her skirts, when they journeyed to see the cliffs and the bridge. It nearly drove her to madness to be out with the stones with so many people around. She only wanted to get back home where she at least had a few walls to afford her protection. Even at home she does not feel safe. She falls asleep holding them in their pouch and wakes with a start, hands feeling the stones through the fabric to be certain they're still there.

She is unfit to manage her household, tend to her child, or fulfill her duties within the branch. Though, aside from standing watch over the Eternal Flame, no one in the branch knows just what their duties are

Nashua's Choice

anymore. Sage Mylas and Apprentice Terridon met with the upper leadership of the branch on the night of the Phoenix's return and ordered them to halt the issuing of ash immediately. The little village of songbirds went quiet, the Great Gate locked. Their patrons from the city clamored outside the Gate for many hours before giving up and going home. It is the same all over, as magic from each branch is suddenly unavailable. Terridon insists on asking Nashua how the branch should preserve the ash and their magic until the Phoenix comes again, or how they should endure their sudden financial crisis. Her reply is always the same: "You decide." She will not discuss it or make decisions the Head should make, nor can she think beyond the stones anyway. Terridon tries to talk to her about the prophecy, Lindall hints around that she should tell him what she's hiding, her mother-in-law asks how they are to survive without opening their amphitheaters to the patrons. Nashua cuts them short because she cannot talk or think about any of it. She can only think about the stones and how she is to keep them safe. She thinks and thinks about her options.

In the end, her true problem is that the Phoenix is telling her what to do. She knows exactly what the Phoenix wants her to do. She hears it loud and clear.

She is just not listening.

Apprentice Terridon comes to their door early that morning. Everyone is up and about. Her mother-in-law, Phaedra, has put away the last of the breakfast dishes and is pulling out the flour for their daily bread. She sets it on the table with a thud. Lindall, dressed for the day and about to leave, is being shadowed by their little son, who follows Lindall down the hall and into their bedroom. Nashua sits stationary by the hearth, the morning fire reduced to glowing coals. She listens to the low, deep sound of Lindall's voice followed by the delighted squeal of their boy. Nashua's hands rest next to her lap, her left hand cupping the place where the stones are hidden in their satchel under her skirts. When the knock comes, her grip tightens.

Phaedra glances at Nashua. When Nashua does not move, Phaedra sighs, brushes the flour off her hands, and answers the door herself. Terridon enters the room as Lindall comes down the hallway, little Dalix riding on his shoulders. The men greet one another as Phaedra goes back to the table and her bread. Dalix pats his hands again and again on his father's head. The two men glance at Nashua as if assessing her ability to handle a conversation.

"Welcome Terridon," she says.

He smiles and comes to her, handing her an envelope. She takes it with her free hand. On the back is the seal of the Order. Instead of opening it she looks to him. "Well?"

Nashua's Choice

"They want to meet with you. We must declare our Head before the funeral so they can approve or deny."

"No. I nominate you."

Terridon says nothing for a moment. "I understand. The Order also wishes to discuss... other things."

Lindall takes half a step closer to them, curiosity drawing him in like a magnet.

Nashua looks at the envelope. She cannot feel the slight trembling of her hand, but the fluttering of the envelope gives it away. The Order has summoned her and she cannot deny them. How is she to do this? The Order has called her. She must go. "When?" she asks.

"This afternoon."

She imagines returning to the Rock of Light with the stones and feels lightheaded.

Her emotions must be written on her face. Terridon says gently, "I can escort you."

"I'll go as well," Lindall says.

Nashua shakes her head. "No," she says. "Apprentice Terridon may take me."

This is met with silence. Even Phaedra stops, hands in the bowl, and watches the scene. Dalix raises both arms and pats the top of his father's head. Pat, pat, pat.

"It's fine," Nashua says, though she feels ill.

The room resumes its motion: Phaedra kneads the dough, Terridon takes his leave, Dalix takes to the floor and toddles to his grandmother, chubby hand extending to request a taste of dough. Nashua drops the envelope on her lap and places her hand on her head. She feels clammy. How is she to go to the Order with the stones?

"Mother," Lindall says. Nashua looks up at the sound of his voice. "Take Dalix for a walk."

Uncharacteristically, Phaedra does not protest. She hears something in his voice as well. Nashua watches Lindall. Lindall stands erect watching the floor. Phaedra covers the dough with a towel to let it rise, washes her hands, and sets Dalix at the table so she can put on his shoes. They exit quickly. Lindall and Nashua listen to their footsteps retreating down the path, to the creaking of the gate, to the sound of their footsteps fading until they disappear.

Lindall comes and rests an elbow on the mantle. She looks up at him, meeting his eyes.

"It's time I know what's going on under my own roof."

She has never been afraid of her husband. She is not afraid now. But she knows when he is determined. Whatever patience he may have shown over the past three days, it is done with now.

She shakes her head and opens her mouth.

"Don't tell me you cannot say!" he says and she flinches like an injured animal. "Enough of this. What is this business?" and he gestures to the bundle under her left hand.

Nashua's Choice

She brings her other hand on top of them and scoots in the chair so the stones are even further away from him.

"Beh!" he says raising his arms and pacing away. "I'm a thief now am I? I have a right to know what's going on with my wife."

"It's to do with the Order. I cannot tell."

"And why do you know anything to do with the Order? You! Not even an Apprentice. Not even a Director," he says hitting his own chest.

The thoughts she has been ignoring for the past three days came back to her now. Here, in this moment, these thoughts that do not seem to be her thoughts press on her more strongly than ever. Again she senses what the Phoenix would have her do. *No*, she thinks. *I don't want to.*

Even in this moment, with her husband broadening his chest and rising in height, as is the way with angry men, Nashua only wants to be here. In her home. In the little village.

Lindall continues to storm but she is not intimidated as she might normally be. She cannot fault him his frustration. Would she feel any differently? She feels an aching tenderness for Lindall she has not felt in a long time. She wants to soothe her husband. She wants to take his hand and bring him to her side.

In spite of the stones, in spite of her weariness, she stands. He scowls at her as she crosses the space between them and lifts one arm to bring him into an embrace. He raises his hands and takes a step back. "Don't try to appease me," he says.

"Lindall, I cannot tell you. I need you to help me."

"Help you with what? All this. Everything. I don't know what's happening. What are you hiding? What is this?" he says gesturing to her necklace, which she instinctively covers with her hand.

His eyes sharpen at this move of secrecy. They both freeze, eyes assessing the other, the clash of their wills becoming a palpable force in the space between them. She takes a step back and he throws up his hands. He is on the move, not for her but for the door. He tears it open and storms down the path. She watches him open the gate and continue on as it slams behind him. She stands there, thighs shaking, door open, until a Chanter comes up the lane and glances toward her. Nashua rushes to the door and pushes it closed. She grips the stones in her left hand, rests her forehead against the door, and listens to the voice of the Phoenix pulsating with the rhythm of her heart: *flee, flee, flee.*

After their son was born, Nashua and Lindall rearranged the furniture in their room to make way for the cradle. They didn't change it back after moving their son to his own room next door, even though the

Nashua's Choice

new arrangement left a loose floorboard partially exposed. One end of the board is concealed by the bed; Nashua placed Lindall's wooden chest over the other end. Even so, every time she steps on the board she feels it give and hears it creak in reply. For the past year she and Lindall have said they should move the furniture back just to spare themselves the constant creaking. For the past year it's gone undone. Nashua stares at the board now, and wonders.

She kneels on the floor, bones aching from exhaustion, and pushes against the chest. She is surprised at her lack of strength. She can only scoot it a bit at a time. If only she could sleep. She moves the chest just enough to uncover the end of the board. She pries at the board with her fingertips. It lifts easily, releasing the scent of dust and moist earth. Underneath is a shallow space between the floor and earth foundation.

She stares at the dark crevice. It is big enough. But should she? She knows she should not waste time wondering. Someone could come home soon. She hovers on the edge of indecision anyway. Her mind is fuzzy with exhaustion. She considers the dark space under the board. Can she really place the stones here and walk away?

Then she remembers why she is here. The Order summoned her and she must go but she will not take the stones with her. She cannot.

She lifts the fabric of her skirts to reveal the satchel and unties the cord keeping the satchel around her waist. It is a coarse, woolen bag with a simple draw opening. It used to contain sewing supplies, which now lie loose on top of Dalix's unfinished winter quilt in the hall chest. She can feel the stones through the material but opens the bag anyway to see them nestled inside. The stones glisten in their pouch. One, two, three. Red, blue, yellow. She runs her fingertips along the top of each stone. She brings her hand to her necklace and outlines the shape of the horn, feels the bumps of each tiny nugget. One, two, three. She repeats this motion again, again, again. The weariness goes down to her bones.

Nashua hears footsteps outside on the path. She jumps as if burned. She stashes the stones in their dark hiding place and slips the board into place. She hears her mother in law open the front door as Nashua crouches against the chest, scooting it back into place. *Phaedra had to have heard that.*

"Nashua?" Phaedra calls down the hall.

Nashua stands as Phaedra crosses the threshold into the room. Dalix is asleep on Phaedra's shoulder.

Phaedra immediately furrows her brows and looks around. "What are you doing?"

"I need my brown wrap," Nashua says.

Phaedra glances at the wrap, draped over a chair in the corner. Nashua goes over to retrieve it. Phaedra sighs and leaves the room. Nashua has no emotion to spare for Phaedra's sighs, which are not uncommon. As far as Phaedra is concerned, Nashua's only redeeming quality is that she delivered a healthy grandson and did not die in childbirth like Lindall's first wife.

Nashua stares at the spot on the floor. This bit of wood protecting their future. She hears Phaedra deposit Dalix on his bed and go down the hall to the kitchen. Nashua stands impotent in the middle of the floor, her left hand clasping her skirt where the stones used to be. She hears Phaedra bang a pot in the kitchen. Nashua should help, but instead she pulls the wrap around her shoulders, sits on the chest, places both feet on the board, and listens to Phaedra prepare lunch alone.

Phaedra clears the midday meal from the table. Nashua distracts herself as best she can with the busy antics of her son, up from his nap. She only managed to eat half of what was on her plate. Phaedra scrapes the remainder into the compost bin with a scowl. Nashua wipes her son's cheeks and stubby hands with a damp rag. Her hands shake slightly. Her mind is on the stones, tucked away in the dark.

Is it enough?

She holds little Dalix on her lap but with the meal over he is squirming away. She would hold him tight to her like the stones if she could, but she knows better. Ever since this child found his feet, he could not be restrained. He slides down her lap, balances on the floor for a moment, then races across the room to his wooden horse. He grabs the little toy that Lindall carved for him for his first birthday and holds it triumphantly in the air. "Horsey!" he says to her. This is a regular game, and she is to say "Horsey" back and neigh with enthusiasm. She cannot muster it today. She gives him a smile and he is satisfied. Horsey's ears go into Dalix's mouth, where they are chewed upon with vigor.

The stones are still in their hiding place.

Nashua sits here at the table as a test. A trial run. How far away can she get without them? She cannot see how she will ever make it all the way to the Rock of Light while the stones stay behind without her.

Phaedra comes to the center of the room, hands on her hips, and eyes on Dalix stumbling around. He is making quick rounds of the place. His energy is boundless.

"We should take him to the gardens," Phaedra announces.

Nashua stands and heads down the hall. "You go," she says, her back to her mother in law.

Phaedra sighs her disapproval. "Come Dalix. Let's go."

After a brief bout of bustling, they leave and the house falls quiet. Nashua lies on top of the floorboard. Sleep takes her in an instant.

Nashua wakes on the floor, the bed looming above her. How long had she slept? She hadn't meant to fall asleep.

A knock sounds at the front door and she realizes this is what woke her. She glances underneath her at the floorboard, wishing she could see the stones to be sure they're still there. She knows they must be, but wishes she could touch them all the same.

Another knock, louder this time. She shuffles down the hall, hands clasped to her stomach, aware of the strange, hunched position she's in but too tired to straighten herself.

She opens the door a crack to see Terridon standing there.

"Am I late?" she asks. She opens the door fully and now sees his wife by his side. She is a tiny redhead with enormous blue eyes.

"No," Terridon answers, "I'm early. We saw Phaedra out with Dalix and thought this might be a good time. Were you sleeping?"

Nashua shrugs.

"We shouldn't have come yet." He knows, surely, how little she sleeps.

She waves his concern away and they linger at the doorway for a moment. She does not know how to talk to him and he doesn't seem sure how to talk to her either. There is so much awkwardness between them these days. His wife breaks the silence with a gentle prompt. "May we come in?"

Of course. Nashua backs away and gestures them in. She is an unfit hostess these days too, along with everything else.

Terridon puts his hand on the small of his wife's back as they come inside and sit on the couch. Nashua sits on the wooden-backed chair opposite them. Terridon takes his wife's hand in his. Nashua looks at her own hands, clasped in front of her. Even her hands look weary.

"Nashua," Terridon begins. She looks at him. "We've come to..." He looks at his wife and they exchange worried glances. *Just tell me,* she is too tired to say. The old Terridon would never have hesitated.

His wife is staring at Nashua's necklace. Nashua covers it with her hand and the woman looks away. Nashua is not trying to be rude. She always has been fond of Terridon's wife.

"We'd like to..." Another aborted attempt from Terridon. He leans forward, the unguarded face of her old friend suddenly before her. Oh how she's missed him. "You trust me," he asks, "don't you?"

She is rocked by his words and his earnest expression, but her reaction is concealed inside herself. She is too weary to move. Her face remains immobile.

"You said I should decide about things," he says. "About the ash?"

She nods.

"I think I know what must be done. I think it will get us through."

"That's good." She does not even sound like herself.

"So you don't need to worry."

She nods. Nodding is easier than talking. Oh, if only she could rest.

"Nashua," he says gently. "We've come to sing for you."

Her throat tightens; she could not speak now even if she tried. She thinks she should protest. There is precious little ash in their possession. She should say no before he wastes any of it on her.

As if reading her thoughts he says, "It is already done."

She is trembling now and glances at his horn necklace, already infused with ash for the song. It's too late to stop him and she is glad. She wants this. She needs it.

Terridon stands and comes near. His wife smiles tenderly. Nashua looks down. Her guilt and gratitude ache within her. Tears, not yet fallen, blur her vision.

Nashua's Choice

Terridon takes her by the hands and draws her up. As he did three days ago, though it may as well have been three years, Terridon takes Nashua by the shoulders and steers her to the couch. She sinks down. Terridon sits on one side, his wife on the other. They each take Nashua by the hands and begin to sing.

She expects the Song of Comfort or the Song of Strength. At the first note she knows she is about to partake of the Song of Openness. Most listeners, even when the listeners are Chanters, tend to put up barriers to this song. It's instinctive. Defensive. It hurts to feel so open. The Song of Openness penetrates these barriers. The listener is cleansed and left an empty vessel, pink and raw. This song is never sung alone; it is always paired with the Song of Healing. These are the most powerful and least requested songs.

Upon hearing the first note, Nashua crumbles. No defensiveness. No resistance. Just beautiful, breathtaking, bitter release. She sobs with her head on her hands, which are clasped with the hands of her healers. She feels Terridon's wife lean into her, hears her sweet song like a whisper in her ear. Terridon squeezes her hand and she squeezes back without ceasing.

They sing; the music and the magic sweep over Nashua until the darkness is expelled and her last tears stand drying on her cheeks.

A brief interlude of silence.

Nashua's Choice

Even before they begin the Song of Healing, she feels peace for the first time in days.

Five

If Nashua didn't know better, she'd think they'd sang the Song of Strength as well. She is more alert, more herself. While her mind is still on the stones and their hiding place, she is able to go with Terridon the long, long way to the Rock of Light. At home, everyone believes that whatever she's hiding is still with her. Even Terridon thinks so. If she must do this thing and leave the stones unguarded, she will at least cover them with a veil of secrecy as well.

On the way to the Rock of Light, she is able to ponder things with far more clarity than she has been able to do for days. She mulls over the prophecy. Much of it is a mystery to her. It seems more a warning to the Order in general and a message to the bearers of the stones in particular than any sort of guidance for her. As she ponders, though, one thing becomes clear to her. If the Phoenix is in danger, it surely is not in any danger right now. Immediately following its regeneration, the Phoenix is at its height of power. No small thing. If the Phoenix requires three defenders, as it clearly thinks it does, it will only require it when it is vulnerable. The only time it is vulnerable is right before it regenerates.

Hundreds of years from now.

The stones may ultimately go into the hands of three defenders, but not for another millennia. How the Phoenix plans to accomplish this, Nashua doesn't know. She only knows that, for now, the stones are hers to guard.

They are gathered in the Cloister, a small stone building built next to the base of the Rock of Light. The Head of the Order sits regally on her cloth covered chair, the center of a semi-circle of chairs in the otherwise bare room. The Order members fill the remaining chairs. One chair is empty; there is a horn embroidered on the back.

Nashua and Apprentice Terridon stand opposite the group. Sage Inne has asked them to declare their new Head. Terridon dives headlong into a resolute explanation of why he thinks it should be Nashua: regardless of who Sage Mylas chose, the Phoenix chose Nashua for something of great significance, and that trumps all. It seems to Nashua that he needs convince no one. Little nodding heads bob up and down the line of Order members.

Nashua's Choice

All but one. Sage Kaleck, Head of the Wysard Branch, is the only one among them with a pondering countenance, the only one who does not seem to have already made up his mind. He is an elderly man whose age has heightened his stance and sense of authority rather than diminished it. His eyes are such a pale blue they are almost colorless. Those pale blue eyes examine Nashua boldly.

She gives up convincing anyone else in the room. The Order's vote must be unanimous. She only needs one person to see things her way. Her husband's words come back to her. *You, not even an Apprentice. Not even a Director.* These words sting, but she wholeheartedly agrees.

Terridon is still going on but Nashua turns to Sage Kaleck, imploring him with her eyes. He must save her from this insanity. What does she know of running a branch? Every person here is her senior by at least twenty years. She does not know what they know, cannot do what so many of them have done.

Sage Kaleck raises his hand to quiet Terridon. "And what say you, Nashua?"

She speaks as if she were speaking to him alone. "I am not even an Apprentice."

"Young Nashua," this from Sage Inne. "The Phoenix sees something in you that you may not. We trust its wisdom and only ask the same of you." Nashua glances at Sage Kaleck as Inne speaks. His face has a neutral expression. Nashua does not know this man;

his face reveals nothing to her. Do they truly all agree? "It is clear to us," Sage Inne continues, "that the Phoenix chose you for something. If not for this, than what?"

Nashua blinks and forgets all about Sage Kaleck. With that one question, she feels herself removed from everyone else in the room. The semi-circle of chairs seem to her to be separated by a great expanse of space and stone floor. Even Terridon, who stands right next to her, seems a great distance from her.

The Phoenix did, indeed, choose her for something.

Nashua knows what it is, and it is not this. It is not to sit in the circle with the Phoenix's chosen leaders. But even they do not know that. The only one in the room who knows what Nashua is to do, is Nashua herself.

She is utterly alone.

The silence drapes over the room like a veil. They wait while she considers Sage Inne's question. Nashua no longer looks to Sage Kaleck for help. She no longer looks to anyone.

She cannot, after all, deny the Phoenix. These good people follow the Phoenix faithfully. It is what the Order and her branches have done for millennia. Nashua must do the same. She is, at last, wrapped in the black cloak of her certainty; she knows what she must do.

Nashua's Choice

"Very well," Nashua says into the emptiness. "I accept."

※ ※ ※

No one moves. She senses Terridon staring at her but she will not look at him. Sage Inne recovers first.

"Well then," and she exhales with a smile. "We are pleased." The group begins to relax, exchanging satisfied looks with one another. "You have chosen wisely Nashua. Let us go forward with boldness."

Indeed, Nashua thinks.

"I, Sage Inne, Head of the Order of Ceinoth and Head of the Eala Branch, elect Nashua to Head of the Cantori Branch. Order members, what say you?"

As one "Yea" vote after another goes down the line, Apprentice Terridon continues to look at her and Nashua continues to ignore him.

All members but one have voted. Attention turns to Sage Kaleck. Nashua senses his hesitation, but he says "Yea" and the moment passes so quickly that it could be argued it never happened at all.

Sage Inne rises from her chair, comes forward, and stops in front of Terridon. She presents a blue horn clasp, the clasp of their branch.

"Apprentice Terridon," Sage Inne says. "On behalf of your branch, please pin this clasp to Nashua's robe."

Sage Inne steps back. Terridon comes around to Nashua's front and their eyes meet at last. It is as it was when she stood in the line in Sage Mylas' room, when the poor man lay coughing and trembling and they all stood on as helpless witnesses. She had exchanged a look with Terridon then, and they understood one another's sorrow in that moment. It is the same now. There is no triumph in Terridon's eyes, no joy in hers.

He furrows his brows at her.

She looks down to the clasp before he can examine her further.

Terridon stands close as he pins the clasp on her robe. "Congratulations," he says, "Sage Nashua."

She suppresses a sigh. It is what it is.

Terridon puts both hands on her shoulders, gives them a reassuring squeeze, and steps away.

"Sage Nashua, please take your place," Inne says, gesturing behind her.

Sage. A most coveted title. Nashua wants nothing of it. She takes a deep breath, lifts her chin, and steps across the room to the chair with the embroidered horn.

They dismiss Terridon to wait for her outside. It is the first time the entire Order has gathered since the arrival of the stones and the prophecy. It is certainly the first time anyone in this room has had the opportunity to discuss these issues with Nashua present. Their meeting is aimless and confused at first. What of the bridge? What of the cliffs? What of the stones from the egg and those on Nashua's horn? The members do not seem to have special insight to the situation any more than Sage Mylas did. The discussion rambles on, full of pontifications, speculations, heated debate, helplessness, and pauses in which everyone regains their strength.

They discuss the prophecy at length. Dissect it bit by bit. They agree with Nashua that the only time the Phoenix is vulnerable to attack is right before it regenerates. This could be anywhere from 600 to 1400 years from now. The Three defenders, whoever they might be, are not even born yet. Nor is whoever plans to attack the Phoenix.

"Who could this be? Who would seek to harm the Phoenix?" asks Sage Kaleck.

"Not just harm, but steal its magic," Sage Inne says. A few members exchange knowing looks. *Who else?* Nashua thinks. "The Citadel of Zevarai would stop at nothing," Sage Inne says.

"They've tried things before," Sage Kaleck agrees.

"Only with us," says another. "Would they go so far?"

"Obviously someone is going to."

The discussion turns to ways to protect the Phoenix—indeed the entire Order and her branches—from members of the Citadel.

Nashua has no desire to listen to more theories. "The Order can spend the next thousand years speculating," she says, "and probably will. It's all guess work. Maybe it's the Citadel. Maybe it's a leader of some group yet to be formed. Maybe it's someone working on their own. We're looking at hundreds of years. Who knows what things will happen in that time?"

"No," Sage Inne says. "We don't truly know how this will play out. We will go to our graves not knowing." Sage Inne pauses a moment, pressed perhaps by the weight of what she just said. "The fact remains, the Phoenix brought us the prophecy and the stones. We must do all we can to proceed with wisdom."

Well, Sage Inne is right about one thing, Nashua thinks. *The prophecy came to the Order, but the stones came to me.*

"If we cannot understand the prophecy just now, we can at least do our part," Sage Kaleck says. "We can guard the stones."

Nashua bristles at this. "*You* guard the stones?"

All eyes are upon her. Sage Inne and Sage Kaleck exchange glances.

Sage Kaleck leans forward in his chair. "Sage Nashua," he says. "Apprentice Terridon tells us you aren't sleeping."

Nashua shrugs.

"You fear for the stones?"

She says nothing.

"They are not safe with you," Sage Kaleck says. "You must know it."

"You may have been the one to retrieve the stones, Nashua," Sage Inne says gently, "but the Order is witness and keeper as well. Our vaults guard the secrets of the Order and can do the same for the Phoenix's stones. It is the only way to keep them safe until they are needed."

Nashua resists the urge to put her hand over her skirt in the place where the stones would have been. She wants them safely in her grasp now more than ever, yet she is exceedingly glad the stones are not here. She glances at Sage Kaleck before addressing Sage Inne.

"With all respect, Sage Inne, I am sure you do not want to attempt to take them from me."

There is a heavy pause before Sage Inne replies, "No one is suggesting such a thing Sage Nashua. But the stones need to be delivered to the Three."

"Yes."

"They won't be born for hundreds of years."

"Most likely. Yes."

Sage Inne and Sage Kaleck exchange glances again. She knows what they're getting at. *Out with it.*

"We will all be dead. *You* will be dead. How can the stones be delivered to the Three if not by the Order? Surely you see. The Order was born of the Phoenix, is sustained by the Phoenix. Who better to protect its secrets? Who better to ensure the Three succeed?"

It only makes sense. Of course it makes sense. But even as she sits here, the feelings that are not her feelings and thoughts that are not her thoughts press on her with power. She will not be turning the stones over to anyone.

Sage Inne seems to think Nashua is relenting. "You need not decide this moment, of course."

Sage Kaleck opens his mouth and Sage Inne raises her hand to still him. "There is time," she nods to him. She looks back to Nashua. "There is time. We can decide how to safeguard it in the vaults. We can decide what enchantments to place upon the records and the stones. Perhaps you will know best how to do this. Perhaps that is your unique role. Nashua, will you ponder how we may best keep these stones safe over the coming centuries?"

Nashua nods. Certainly she will ponder, but not in the way they think. Nashua says nothing. More than at any other time during this meeting, silence is her best protection. Let them think what they want.

"Good," Sage Inne says. "I think we have discussed enough for one day."

Sage Kaleck clears his throat in some sort of protest.

"There is time," Sage Inne says again. "Let us adjourn so we may prepare for the morrow. Our dear friend."

Many heads nod with regret and Nashua herself looks down to her hands in her lap. Her beloved Sage.

"Let us meet again in four days. Is that agreeable?"

So soon, Nashua thinks. After a few nods and a general silent assent, Sage Inne rises. "Then let us rest."

Just like that, Nashua is released.

Terridon and Nashua return to the little village through the Great Gate and exit the carriage near the courtyard. It is early evening, but these spring days are long and the sun won't set for a few more hours yet. The Courtyard of Songs is lit up but it all looks strange and lonely. The flowers still put forth their colorful displays and the fountains still sing their songs. The amphitheaters, however, are quiet and the courtyard is otherwise bare.

As she and Terridon cross the courtyard she sneaks a glance at the profile of her friend. His boyish face carries the mark of both wisdom and kindness. He is graying around the temples and fine lines hint at deeper wrinkles to come. She often forgets his age and tends to overlook it in his features.

She wishes she could tell him what's going to happen. She wishes she could ask him for advice. As they ascend the steps to Marion Hall, Nashua thinks, *Everything is lost to me already.*

They enter the building, as lifeless and deserted as the courtyard had been. "The Apprentices will be waiting in the Assembly Room," Terridon says, and turns down a hall in that direction.

Nashua continues straight ahead. "I'll be there shortly."

She hears Terridon stop and trot up to her. "Where are you going?"

"Home."

"But we must make the announcement."

"Yes, I know," she says. "I will meet you there." She is not doing anything until she checks on the stones. It has been long enough. Now that she is so close to home, she is becoming agitated for them.

"But what should I say to them?"

Nashua stops and turns to face Terridon. He has so frequently been frustrated with her lately. He will be even more unhappy with her soon enough, but what can she do?

"Apprentice Terridon?"

"Yes, Sage Nashua."

She manages not to cringe at the title. Sage indeed. "You may tell them whatever you feel best. I leave it to you."

Nashua's Choice

Terridon furrows his brow at her. She does not look away. How she is going to miss him. "And," he says slowly, "what of our accounts?"

It is an irrelevant question at this moment. There is the announcement to make this evening, then the funeral tomorrow. There will be no discussion of financial remedies or any other such business until the following day, at the earliest. She knows full well Terridon asks her this as a test. He wants to see her answer.

She considers giving him the same answer she has given him for days, "You decide." It's what it will come down to anyway. Instead she says, "We will discuss it after the funeral."

His expression has not changed one whit and he continues to furrow his brow at her.

Stop trying to puzzle me out, she thinks. *Stubborn man.* "Go into the Assembly Hall or wait for me here if you wish. I'll be back shortly."

She turns and begins walking away.

"And we will make the announcement then?"

She does not stop but waves her hand. "Yes. We'll do it then."

He says no more and does not follow her. She does not turn to see if he is still standing there or has moved along.

She exits Marion Hall to the rear and passes one residence after another. A few Chanters are about and they cast her curious glances. She does not slow her pace or give anyone a look that might suggest it's safe to approach her. Her need to see the stones increases with each step. She resists the urge to run for the house outright.

She goes through the garden gate, up the path, opens the door, home at last. The smell of Phaedra's bread fills the house. It is cooling on the table, alongside a bowl of greens, while Phaedra stirs at a big pot on the stove. It smells like her creamy cabbage and haddock soup. She stops and looks at Nashua expectantly.

Phaedra is waiting, like everyone else, to hear the news but Nashua has no interest in that. "Where's Lindall?" Nashua asks. She could assume, but wants to know for certain.

"At the Assembly Hall."

"Dalix?"

There is no need for Phaedra to answer as Dalix has come toddling down the hall at the sound of his mother's voice. His flyaway hair is sticking up in the back; a remnant, no doubt, from his afternoon nap. He reaches for her and she scoops him into her arms.

"Will you please send for Lindall?" Nashua says. "I must speak to him."

Phaedra huffs. "Weren't you just there?"

"No."

"Haven't they made the announcement?"

"Not yet."

Nashua's Choice

Phaedra turns to the chopping block where a few peeled carrots and a knife await her. Nashua glances down the hall and toward her bedroom. She wonders if Dalix can feel her heart pounding against her chest. She needs to see those stones.

"I don't have time to fetch Lindall *and* finish dinner," Phaedra says. Her entire body shakes as she takes to the carrots with vigor. *Chop, chop, chop. Chop, chop, chop.* "I can't do everything. You'll have to get him yourself or wait for him to come home."

She smacks down the knife, gathers up the carrots, and tosses them into the bowl of greens on the table. "Dinner will be ruined with all this waiting if they don't hurry up about it."

The burden of Nashua's unhelpfulness is magnifying Phaedra's naturally fretful disposition, and Nashua regrets that she has left her to do all the work alone, but she has no thought to spare for it just now. She needs to get to the stones. "*Mother*," Nashua says firmly. Phaedra startles, perhaps at the tone, perhaps at the word. "Go get your son."

Phaedra blinks at her. "Hmpf," she says staring.

Dalix wiggles out of Nashua's arms and heads to the table to investigate. Nashua does not take her eyes from Phaedra.

"Hmpf," Phaedra says again. She removes the towel around her waist and tosses it on the table. "I have nothing else to do," she says, but more to herself than to Nashua. Neither one of them tries to stop Dalix, who has climbed onto the bench and is reaching into the bowl of greens, seeking a slice of carrot. Nashua watches Phaedra leave, scowl and all, but does not move until she hears the latch at the garden gate.

Nashua hustles down the hall and into their bedroom. She glances around as she crosses to the chest, looking for signs of disturbance. All seems well but it is not until she moves the chest, lifts the board, and sees the pouch with its familiar bulges that she exhales the breath she'd been holding in. She takes the bag, feels the stones, opens the pouch.

They wink up at her.

She holds them to her chest with shaking hands as her heart rate reluctantly slows back to normal. Such a brief but sharp moment of panic. Now that she has them in her hands she doesn't want to put them back, but she has thought everything through. She spent the carriage ride back to the little village laying her plans. She will remove the stones when it is time.

As she replaces the stones and the board, she hears Dalix coming down the hall. He appears in the doorway. She gets to her feet and puts her hands on both hips, inspecting him. He is holding two or three carrot slices in each hand while he munches away on another in his mouth. He grins up at her. For a moment she is just Nashua again. Not Head of the branch. Not Keeper of the stones. In this glorious moment of normality, Nashua is just the mother to this

Nashua's Choice

silly little boy. She laughs and picks him up. "Little goat," she says, heading back to the kitchen.

She reaches the living room and hears the garden gate open and close. She stops in the middle of the room.

The moment is over.

※ ※ ※

Phaedra enters first and goes straight to the pot to check her soup. "Did you stir it at all?"

Lindall stops on the threshold, door open. He wears a scowl that resembles his mother's and Nashua sees in an instant he has not forgotten their exchange this morning. Terridon makes an appearance at the gate, apparently investigating the delay. "Everything alright?" he calls.

"We'll be right there," Nashua calls back, unable to hide her irritation. She needs to talk to Lindall alone. Terridon frowns but takes the hint and leaves.

Phaedra has her own irritations. She spies Dalix stuffing another carrot into his mouth. "It's late," Phaedra says. "The child is hungry."

Nashua deposits Dalix on the floor. "Go ahead and eat. Lindall and I need to talk."

"Everyone's waiting in the Assembly Hall," Lindall says. He will not even come inside.

Phaedra slices the bread while Dalix climbs onto the bench. Nashua does not want to have this conversation in front of Phaedra. It's Lindall she needs to convince. Once Lindall is on board, Phaedra will go along. Nashua takes a few steps back, intending they talk privately in the bedroom. She gestures that Lindall should follow her.

"If you wanted to tell me yourself," he says, "I already know."

She stops. "Know what?"

"That you're the new Head."

"Oh." *That.*

Phaedra stops her slicing and stares. Lindall continues to scowl.

"I..." Nashua says.

Phaedra sets the knife on the counter out of reach and Dalix reaches for bread. The activity in the kitchen goes on, with Phaedra keeping one eye on her son and his wife, but Nashua and Lindall merely stand there.

Nashua feels the Phoenix warning her but she doesn't need it. She feels the warning in her own heart. The look on Lindall's face tells her everything. There is no relenting in this man. Nashua knows there will be no appeasing him, no calming him, no convincing him to follow her without knowing the reason why, no future time when he will stop wondering what she's hiding. He will always want to know.

She cannot tell Lindall anymore than he already knows, but he will not follow her without knowing.

Even if he did know, whose side would he be on? Would he help her hide? Would he guard her and her secret? Or would he side with the Order, tell them of her plans, and try to stop her? Can she risk even asking him?

"Everyone is waiting," he says again.

She nods. She will have to keep pretending. Even with him.

She fears her knees will buckle with the weight of what this means. She must leave without him.

Six

As they walk back to Marion Hall, Lindall marches ahead. Nashua knows she cannot delay. She senses the urgency of the Phoenix. It is almost as if it wants her to retrieve the stones, leave the little village and not look back, right this very minute. But it never occurred to her that she would have to leave without her husband. What will she do? Where will she go on her own? And what about Dalix? She looks at her husband, several paces ahead of her, his anger palpable even from behind. What about their son? Whatever Lindall lacks as a husband, he makes up for as a father. How can she take his child away?

Her heart pounds in her chest as if she is fleeing this very moment. As if she could be caught this very moment. As if...

Nashua's pace slows. The distance between her and Lindall increases.

The pounding in her chest intensifies. As if she is under threat.

Nashua stops. Lindall goes through the rear door of Marion Hall and does not notice she is not behind him.

She can hardly breathe.

The stones.

Nashua bolts to the house, through the gate, through the door, glancing in the living room, hallway, kitchen —all empty—while streaking down the hall toward her bedroom.

Phaedra is on the floor next to the bed, her legs twisted strangely under her as if she crumpled where she stood, one arm stretched out with the red stone resting in her open palm. Her eyes are open and glassy. Even before Nashua rushes to the body and falls to her knees, even before she shakes her and calls her name, she knows Phaedra is gone. The red stone glints darkly.

It will not be stolen, she thinks. The thing killed her...

Her thoughts stop sharply. She looks about frantically and takes it all in: the board is on the floor, the hole empty, the pouch lies next to Phaedra empty. Nashua slaps her hand on top of the pouch in desperation. The blue stone lies just under the bed, as if it fell and slid, but the yellow one is nowhere to be seen.

Nashua's Choice

She hears Dalix's toddling run and spins in time to see him disappear down the hallway toward the living room. She scrambles to her feet, rushes down the hallway, and comes to an abrupt halt.

There he stands, holding the yellow stone in his chubby hand and banging it against the edge of the table. *Bang, bang, bang.* He squeals in delight.

Nashua cannot move, for she understands what this magic is. The stones cannot be stolen. Dalix is only alive because he has no thought of keeping the stone from her. Her very skin is on edge as her fear and urgency wrestle within her. "Dalix." Her voice does not sound like her own. "Bring it here honey."

The stone goes to his mouth and her heart stops. A sound like "no" escapes her.

She takes a careful step forward and sees his face light up with the game. He is going to run with it. She retreats. She thinks of the only word he knows to obey. "Hot."

Dalix points to the hearth. "Hot."

"Yes. Hot stone. Drop it."

He toddles around the table, laughing. She approaches, closing the gap. She kneels so she can look under the table to better see him. He drops the stone and it lands next to the wall, away from her. He bends to pick it up before she can move.

"Bring it to momma," she says. "Bring it here son."

He throws it toward her, a new game. His aim is bad and it goes wide, out of both of their reaches. For the first time, something overrides her instinct to protect the stones. She lunges for Dalix and brings him into her arms away from danger. "Good boy."

Legs shaking, she holds his soft body close, smelling his smell, cupping her hand over the back of his head. He wraps his chubby arms around her neck and squeezes before squirming under her grip. He is ready to fetch the stone and play again, but she grabs a slice of Phaedra's bread and hands it to him. He chews happily, the stone forgotten.

She sets him on the bench, rushes for the stone, and runs down the hallway. Phaedra's crumpled body is a shock but Nashua does not slow until she's retrieved the other two stones. "Oh Phaedra," she says as her shaking hands struggle to conceal the stones in their pouch. "Oh Phaedra, I'm so sorry."

She hears Dalix toddling down the hallway. Hears the front door open. Hears Lindall calling, "Nashua?"

Nashua lifts her skirts and fumbles for the waist cord. Dalix comes through the door and stops. His smile vanishes and his little face searches hers. Tears for her mother-in-law stain Nashua's cheeks and she takes one step back after another as she tries to tie the pouch to the cord.

Lindall's heavy steps resound down the hallway as he calls, irritated as ever, "Nashua!"

She ties the knot and drops her skirts over the entire assembly as he rounds the corner, sees what she was doing, sees his mother, halts, and turns a pale shade of gray.

"Mother?"

"I'm so sorry."

Dalix, who stands between his father and the scene, looks up in confusion. He reaches up but Lindall steps around him and into the room.

"MOTHER!" He drops to his knees, grabs her shoulders, face, arms.

Dalix starts to cry.

"Oh Lindall, I'm so sorry."

Hunched over his mother, Lindall's head snaps up and he gives Nashua a crazed look. *"What did you do?"* Dalix's cries turn frantic.

She shakes her head. He glances at her skirt, at the place where the stones are hidden. She backs up as Lindall stands. "No."

"What did you do to her?"

More steps down the hallway and Terridon appears at the door. "What's going on?"

It seems that every person in the room is making noise at that point. Lindall is railing, accusing her. Dalix is screaming. Nashua is climbing over the bed to get away from Lindall and find a clear path for the door, saying again and again, "It wasn't me, it wasn't me." Terridon is nothing but halting exclamations of "Oh!" and "Stop!" and "What?" as he takes in the commotion and poor Phaedra lying dead in the middle of it.

Nashua bolts for the door and tries to push past Terridon but it's no use with Lindall crying "Stop her!" and Terridon holding her fast. Like a caged animal she struggles to get out of his grip but Terridon says in her ear, "Steady, steady." She hears her poor child screaming and tries to pull away again. Again she hears Terridon's voice in her ear, firmer this time, "Be still Nashua." She stops resisting though the urgency to flee does not leave her. Terridon turns so he is between her and Lindall but does not let her go. "I have her," he says to Lindall. "I have her. What happened?"

Lindall turns to his mother, gesturing, and his panic seems to leave him. He hunches over, deflated. He kneels and cradles Phaedra's head in his arms.

Terridon slowly releases Nashua as she bends down for her crying son. Dalix clings to her and hides his face in her neck. "Shhhh, now. Shhhh." He stops crying but continues to whimper.

Nashua longs to comfort her husband, to put her arms around him, but she will not take another step into that room. "Lindall, I found her that way."

He remains on the floor but turns to Terridon, face hard. "GET HER OUT OF HERE!"

Two Apprentices come through the door and Nashua tries to flee again but Terridon restrains her. The commotion surrounds her with Lindall shouting for her to leave, more Apprentices coming into the house—fed up with waiting or drawn by the shouting—all making noise at once with their questions, and

Nashua's Choice

Nashua trying to comfort her child while Terridon escorts her down the hall. With Nashua out of his sight, Lindall stops his shouting but his wailing takes over instead. It is all chaos and noise and confusion until Terridon's voice booms through the house: "ENOUGH!"

A stunned silence falls upon the company. Even Dalix looks at him wide eyed.

Terridon points at an Apprentice, "You see to Lindall," and another, "You fetch the physician," and another, "Send the physician to me after he's examined Phaedra. We'll be in my office." Even in her distraught state, Nashua is taken by Terridon's authority and efficiency. No matter what the Order said, she knows who her Sage is.

Another Apprentice lingers near the door. "What about the announcement?"

Terridon looks at him in disbelief. "Dismiss the rest. We have enough to deal with tonight."

🙭 🙭 🙭

Terridon's office is located in the east wing of Marion Hall and has a window facing the courtyard leading to Meadowlark Gate. There is a small desk, three chairs, a bookcase, two wall lanterns, and a faded mural of the sea. After Nashua explained what

Nashua's Choice

happened with Phaedra and she gets Dalix to fall asleep on her shoulder, they wait together in silence.

The physician comes shortly. Terridon talks to him through the slightly open door, blocking Nashua from view. "It appears to be a heart attack," Nashua hears the man say. "No sign of... violence."

"Of course not. How is Lindall?"

"Better. He wants Nashua and his boy to come home."

"Thank you."

Terridon shuts the door and turns to Nashua. "Well," he says, "you can go back now."

She nods but does not move. Dalix sleeps on her shoulder. The only time she can hold this child for more than a minute is when he's sleeping like this. She relishes the feel of his soft body against hers and cannot bear the thought of letting him go. She cannot seem to look away from his face, his round cheeks, his little nose and long eyelashes. What will he look like as a young boy? What will he look like as a man? She will never know, for she cannot take him with her.

Nashua has a vague sense that in a practical way, he is better off here. There is the concern about how she will survive on her own, let alone with a child, whereas here, at least, he would be safe, sheltered, fed, loved.

But it is more than that. If it were only that, she would find a way.

In the end, she knows there is truly only one thing keeping her from bringing her child with her: the stones. What if, one day, he finds them as Phaedra did? What if he had it in his heart to keep them? She sees the image of Phaedra's dead body on the floor and knows it could've been her son. Could be, in the future. Oh she could not bear it.

How cruel that Dalix's best chance of survival is to leave him here, without a mother to love him, for who could ever love as a mother could? She squeezes him again.

"Terridon, will you do me a favor?"

The tears run freely down her cheeks.

"Take Dalix home. He needs to rest in his own bed. I'll... I'm not ready to go back yet." He studies her. "Lindall, you know. Talk to Lindall and see how he's doing? Then you can come back and tell me it's really okay to go home. Is that alright? Can you do that for me?"

She still has not handed Dalix over. She said it. She decided it. But she cannot let her boy go.

But oh help me, he's not safe with me.

"You want me to take him home?"

Nashua nods. "Make sure Lindall's alright."

Terridon studies her.

"Please."

"Yes." He pats her shoulder. "Yes, Nashua. Of course."

He reaches for Dalix and she tries to smile as she lifts her boy away and watches Terridon settle him onto his shoulder. She roughly brushes the tears out of her eyes so she can see his little face. "Sweet boy," she says, kissing him on the cheek. "Mama loves you," she says kissing him again. One arm hangs down and she grabs his little hand, squeezes it, and kisses it too.

"Are you sure you want me to take him?" Terridon asks.

"No," she says shaking her head. "But go quickly. Go."

And he does. Just like that Terridon leaves and closes the door behind him and Dalix is gone. Nashua leans against the door, tight fists against her forehead, muting her cry so Terridon doesn't hear her and come back.

Nashua lingers. She remembers she had a plan, but she can't think what it was. All she can think is her most immediate step, *Out the door, out the gate. Out the door, out the gate.*

It is some time before her body obeys. She wipes her cheeks dry, takes a deep, shuddering breath. Another calmer breath.

Out the door, out the gate.

It is like a chant.

Out the door, out the gate.

She opens the door. She pokes her head out, looking first in one direction, then the other. The hall is empty. The exit to the courtyard is not far. She goes into the hallway, to the door leading outside, opens it, and is in the courtyard. The sun is low on the horizon and dusk will be upon her shortly. She doesn't have much light left.

She stands there a moment, mind empty.

Out the gate.

She crosses the courtyard. No one about. No one to stop her. They are all in their homes, or perhaps in hers. Talking over the evening's events. Gathering around Lindall and his mother. Gossiping. Speculating. It will be a long night.

She comes to the gate and stops. *Out the gate.* She lingers and places her hands on the stones hidden under her skirts.

"Nashua?"

She spins and sees Terridon standing in the courtyard, just arm's reach away. No Dalix. No one else. She nearly bolts but he raises his hand, "It's okay. Here." He takes a pack off his shoulder and holds it out to her. "For the journey."

She is both surprised and not surprised that he has figured her out. She doesn't know whether to make up a story and deny, or just give in. Her departure is supposed to be done in secret, but Terridon knows the other secrets too, doesn't he? She stares at the pack with indecision.

"You can't leave empty handed. It isn't much but it should see you for a while." He steps closer and opens the top flap. She can't see everything inside, for it's a decent-sized pack, but on top she sees some rations—

three apples, a bundle of dried meat, a tin of some sort—and a hunting knife in a leather sheath.

She remembers her plans now, all gone awry. She had a mental list of all she'd pack and how they'd travel with only the most necessary items. They have a little money set aside, and she had her grandmother's ring that she could sell if they got desperate. She was going to walk away without any of it, not even a scrap of food.

"I'm afraid it's not very thorough," Terridon says. "I realized on my way back to you that I'd forgotten a lantern. The water pouch is only half full."

How long has he known?

"When did you do this?"

"Just now. I was afraid I'd miss you."

"What about Dalix?"

"I ran into Apprentice Ulia. She took him home. Otherwise I would've packed one handed."

And he would've come back with Dalix. She wishes she could've seen his little face one last time, but doesn't know if she could bear another goodbye.

Terridon has refastened the top flap but she still hasn't taken the pack. She needs to get away but it's like cutting off her own arm. It's so hard to bring down the knife.

"Nashua," he says quietly. He comes to her, slides the pack onto her back, adjusts the straps, and puts his hands on her shoulders. "I'm so sorry."

There is nothing she can say to that.

"Do you know where you're going?"

"Yes."

"Are you sure they won't be able to find you?"

She shrugs. "Let us hope."

He nods.

She knows she can't linger. She has spent too much time already. She takes a step back and he doesn't follow her.

"Watch over him," she says. "Make sure he knows his mother loves him."

"I will."

"Try to help Lindall understand. Tell him I'm sorry."

"I will."

She lingers a minute more.

"Don't forget me."

He shakes his head. "I won't."

And that is all she can stand. She steps through the gate, closes the latch behind her, and crosses the road into the field on the other side. She doesn't look back. Now that she is moving, now that it is done, she focuses on the only thing left to her: getting the stones to safety. She heads for a thicket of shrubs, which are soon enough between her and the walls of the little village. She gets to the far end of the field and reaches a path that will lead her to the road that will take her east. On one side of the path is a tiny house next to a sprawling orange grove. A small boy plays on the porch but he pays Nashua no mind and she avoids looking at him as well. She walks as quickly as she can without drawing attention to herself and soon enough she is on the road that goes east. Her original plans were to leave by night, so as to go unseen, but the little village lies in between the city and open country so she does not have far to go before she is away from people and hidden by her isolation.

Nashua realizes she hasn't had dinner but she finds the idea of eating repulsive and continues on. The Cliffs of the Realm are to her back as she heads in the opposite direction anyone would think to look for her. The familiar road soon takes her to new territory—valleys she does not recognize, hillocks she does not know. She did not realize these strange lands were so close to home. Though she has not walked long, they make her feel far away from everything she knows, as if she is in a new country already.

Without another soul to call upon and without the ash to lend its potency, Nashua sings herself a song. The Song of Comfort is diminished, but familiar, and eases her way down the darkening road.

Excerpt from GIFT OF THE PHOENIX

Find out what happens when Nashua delivers the stones to their rightful bearers in my full-length novel, GIFT OF THE PHOENIX. Nashua plays a brief but crucial role in the first two chapters.

The old woman looked like a piece of fruit left to rot in the sun. Corren watched her cross the grounds of Tower Hall South, home to a clandestine group of wizards and their pupils. Unknown visitors were uncommon, but she drew his attention for more reasons than that. He had been extracting finger root with a single word, *enbiree*, and collecting it in a woolen bag. The appearance of this woman caused him to stop mid movement. He stood under a hickory tree, the bag lying forgotten at his feet.

She drew near, her brittle hair yellowed in the sun. Now he noticed her eyes. One was brown, the other blue. He found it uncomfortable to look at her, as if he were staring impolitely at her oddity, but neither could he look away. She shuffled under the canopy of the tree, her frame darkened by shadow, and stopped. She was here for him, a fact he somehow knew the moment he saw her.

"Corren of Landsdowne," she said.

Just as this stranger's presence was out of the ordinary, so too was this greeting. It had been years since he was "Corren of Landsdowne." No one from that village would know to look for him here.

Memories flashed through his mind: Corren watching Mother Taiven collapse in front of Tower Hall South on their way home to Landsdowne... wizards and witches swarming around her body and ushering him inside their stone halls... the echoing of their voices as he heard phrases like "what do we do with him?" and "who would take on an eight-year-old boy?" Even now, Corren was amazed at how sharply he could recall the memory of himself, orphaned for the second time in his life, huddled on a narrow bed in an empty room, not knowing what would become of him, not yet knowing it was Aradia who would save him. It was a turning point in his childhood. Aradia had knelt by his bed—her long silvery hair and powerful presence a contrast to her young age—and asked him "will you allow me to care for you?" He knew at that moment that nothing could harm him if she decided to keep him safe. So he stayed. Magic had permeated every aspect of his life since then, a skill that came so natural to him it felt akin to fate. Even before he was of age,

Aradia selected him to be one of her apprentices. Despite his promise to himself that he would find his parents someday, in the thirteen years following Mother Taiven's death, he never did make it back.

So why was this woman calling him "Corren of Landsdowne"?

"You know me?" he asked, unable to tame his eagerness.

The woman nodded. "Once. Long ago."

He took a step forward. She was too aged to be his mother, but perhaps... "Are you my grandmother?"

Her strange eyes saddened. "No, boy. I bring you news of a different sort."

Her answer stung and he realized the yearning for his family had never lessened—it had only been buried. He regretted his rashness. It was not like him to be so unguarded. "What news?" he asked, trying to recover a sense of formality.

She did not reply, only stretched out her frail hand. Shining in her palm was a red stone. "Take it," she said. As if there were nothing else he could have done, he did.

It was rectangular, nearly as long as his hand and half as wide, coming to a soft point at both ends. Its scarlet color was captivating. He wrapped his fingers around its smooth surface and everything fled from his consciousness. All he knew was the stone and himself holding it. A jolt raced up his arm. As abruptly as it came the feeling fled. He opened his hand. The stone looked harmless enough, but his palm tingled and heart pounded. Something inside him was different. Something he did not know had been sleeping, started to awake.

"Show it to no one," the old woman said, and he startled. Her voice pulled him back into the world. "*Tell* it to no one," she said. "Come see me in a month, exactly."

"What is it?" He did not mean to whisper.

She did not answer, only gave him directions to her home... in Landsdowne.

"How do you know me? Who are you?"

She was already turning to leave. "You will know more than you want to soon enough." She left the shadow of the tree and slowly crossed the grass with the concentrated walk of the elderly. He watched her only for a moment, his vision drawn to the stone. He felt as if part of him were sliding into its depths. He closed his fist around the stone and held it protectively to his chest.

He knew he should embrace caution. Unknown magic could be dangerous, deadly even. He watched the old woman disappear around a building. He feared neither the woman nor the stone. Did that make him a fool? He began to consider how, in a month's time, he would sneak away to Landsdowne, without Aradia knowing the reason why.

Nicolai had never been this close to a wizard before. It was almost enough to distract him from recent events. Almost.

It was a strange thing to see a wizard pulling water from Nicolai's own well. He was clearly parched, for he filled his cup with the ladle and drank it down in nearly one gulp. Travelling long, no doubt. Nicolai wanted to ask why a wizard couldn't just conjure up some water, but decided against it.

"I should've brought more water," the wizard said. "I wasn't expecting such a long journey today."

"Help yourself," Nicolai said and extended his hand. "I'm Nicolai of Knobby Tree."

He shook it wearily. "Corren of Tower Hall South."

Corren the wizard was tall, nearly as tall as Nicolai, and held himself with the surety of someone who took self-confidence for granted, though Nicolai sensed no air of superiority either. His sharp features and dark hair added to his rather serious countenance, but all this was softened by his clear blue eyes and polite manner. He wore a cloak of fine linen, tightly woven, soft from the looks of it.

He was not the first traveler to make use of their well, though certainly the most interesting. Their well was situated not far from the road leading from Stonebridge to South Caedmonia. The road ran along his family's homestead on one side, neighbors to the west bordered another, and the other two sides were hemmed in by the Wilds. Nicolai's family had farmed their land in the shadow of the Wilds for ten generations. Local farmers of Knobby Tree thought it an unfortunate plot: cursed for its location. It was so undesirable that even if Nicolai's family wanted to sell no one would buy it. Nicolai thought this foolish considering the fact that their soil was known to be fertile (at least in recent years), but this was not enough to dispel the fear of generations. Nicolai's father was never much bothered by the presence of the Wilds, but when Nicolai was a child his mother sent him out to play with the admonition not to go into the trees.

Corren sighed and wiped his brow. It was a warm autumn day, but Nicolai preferred it to working in the summer heat. It mattered less now that the harvest was finally over. "Traveling long?" Nicolai asked.

"Well, I thought I was going to... to a meeting in Landsdowne, but as soon as I got there I was sent straight back out. Now I'm going to Stonebridge just to fetch a pot for a little old lady." The wizard glanced at Nicolai and shrugged as if to say he wasn't bothered by it.

Nicolai knew better. He smiled. "Elders can be demanding that way."

"I suppose." Corren took another drink, tipping his head back to empty the cup, and set the ladle on the rim of the well.

"If you've a flask I'll fill it for you."

"I was going to ask. Thank you."

Corren and Nicolai grabbed the ladle at the same time, pulled away together, and inadvertently knocked it down the center of the well. Nicolai dove for it, catching the end of the handle with the tips of his fingers before grabbing it with his other hand.

"That was close," he said, depositing it into the bucket. His stomach smarted from where he had crushed it against the well. Corren was staring in astonishment, not at Nicolai, but at his shirt. Nicolai followed his gaze with a glance and his heart tightened. His necklace had come out and the yellow stone attached to it glinted in the sun. Nicolai shoved it back under his shirt, his heart pounding in his ears. Corren was filling his water flask as if nothing had happened at all. Nicolai thought he saw the wizard's hands shaking.

"Well," Corren said, glancing at him without quite meeting his eyes. "I thank you for your hospitality. I'd best be on my way."

Nicolai nodded a farewell. Corren had noticed the stone, there was no doubt about that, and Nicolai questioned the wisdom of wearing it. *But what else am I to do with this thing?*

Nicolai felt sure he would be seeing Corren again, and his sense of foreboding only increased when the wizard headed not for Stonebridge, but back the way he'd come.

The day the woman visited Nicolai, he had been clearing the ditch in the west field. Rain had clogged it with debris and the water broke a groove through the side of the trench. She came along the edge of the corn stalks that stood well over her head: the last corn days away from harvesting. He first thought she was a stranger to the area and likely lost. He wondered how someone so feeble looking came to be traveling alone. Perhaps she wasn't lost but had a companion who was hurt and needed help. He tried to anticipate her reason for being there, but by the time she was next to him he found himself waiting for her to speak. Something about this woman stilled him. It may have been her eyes, the one brown and one blue making it difficult to know which one to look at. Still, something else caused him to look at her as if he already knew she had been coming.

"You are Nicolai," she said, not as a question.

He cocked his head. "Do I know you?"

"Hmm," she said, "I suppose the answer to that is 'no.' But I know *you*, and I'm here to give you what is yours."

She held out a hand, her skin mottled with sun spots. In her palm was a stone. It was such a luminous yellow he squinted to look at it. She held it out, but he did not take it.

"That is not mine," he said, wondering how she could think it was.

"It belongs to you," she said nodding.

"I think you've made a mistake."

"I'm sure I haven't." She took his hand.

"But I've never seen…" She placed the stone in his palm, released him, and his words died in his mouth. It was cool to the touch as a gem is cool, but he realized at once this was no mere gem. There was something else within it, something he could not see, but could feel. His fingers curled inward, the stone cradled in his hand. When his grasp was complete, a sensation ignited in his palm, shot up his arm, and caused him to jerk in surprise. He gaped at her.

She leaned in, her eyes holding his. "It is yours."

Despite her admonition to keep the stone a secret, he had no intention of hiding such a thing from his father. After she had gone, he went toward his father working in the north field. Nicolai began with a walk but after a few steps burst into a run.

Nicolai stood over his father by nearly a head. Nicolai told him what happened, still holding the stone and catching his breath.

Graham furrowed his brows at the stone, which Nicolai held close as if afraid something was going to happen to it. "How did she know your name?"

"I don't know. She never told me hers, now I think of it."

"You didn't ask?"

Nicolai thought back on the conversation. It had been peculiar, like a dream, or something that happened without his feet quite on the ground. "No."

Graham looked around, scanning for her. There was only the field, the house, the road. "Why would a stranger give you something so valuable?" he asked. "Do you think it was stolen?"

Nicolai dropped his eyes to the stone. He felt part of him sinking into its center, while the rest of him stood rooted to the earth. The stone pulled at Nicolai. If he should have been alarmed by this, he wasn't. The old woman had said it was his. Against all reason Nicolai believed her. "No," he said. "I don't think it's stolen."

Nicolai felt an urge to leave and tightened his fingers around the stone.

"Nicolai? What's wrong?"

Nicolai shook his head. He felt he needed to run, but his mind fought against it. He told himself to calm down. Why did he feel fear?

Graham looked at Nicolai in concern. His eyes dropped to the stone, and he pressed his lips together. "I... don't know... if you should keep that."

It took all Nicolai's will to fight the urge to run from his father. Perhaps he *should* fear the stone. Perhaps there was dark magic in it. What else would bring on such emotion? But Nicolai didn't fear the stone. He feared his father. His father who he loved, his father who had never harmed him. Still, he needed to run. Escape. But Nicolai would not allow his feet to do it. He would not run from his father.

His face must have betrayed something of this.

"What's wrong?" Graham asked. "What is it?" He leaned in and Nicolai flinched back.

Graham straightened in surprise.

Nicolai brought the stone up, pressed it to his chest with both hands. His father's eyes locked on it.

"Drop the stone, son."

"No." His voice sounded far away but was firm. He had to run. Flee. Run *now*. He felt these thoughts would crush him if he did not obey. His father's eyes were on the stone; his face resolute. Nicolai saw as if in slow motion, Graham's hand rising, his aim on the stone.

Nicolai let go his will.

Time caught up in a rush. His legs reacted but it was too late. His father's hand was already there. Nicolai jerked away in a panic, his arm flinging back and his father lunging after it. The two men stumbled, Nicolai backward and Graham ramming into Nicolai's chest as he stretched for the stone, both their eyes on it, the impact and uncertain footing bringing them to the ground. Nicolai lost the advantage of height.

As Nicolai hit the ground he saw his father's hand close around his own, and around the stone. A yellow light flashed out of the stone and Nicolai clenched his eyes shut. His father crashed on top of him, not moving. Nicolai jerked the stone away and the light withdrew.

Graham felt like dead weight. Nicolai, panting, held him and rolled him onto the ground. He feared his father had hit his head and hoped he had only passed out. Still seeing flashes from the light, Nicolai blinked his eyes furiously, pulling himself up to kneel next to his father. That was when his sight cleared and he saw his father's face: his mouth hung open, his eyes staring at nothing.

Everything around Nicolai pressed in on him, turning to blackness. The screams he heard, he would later learn, belonged to his mother who had come out to the field. But to his ears and to his stricken mind her screams were nonexistent, indistinguishable from his own. Every part of him cried out as he clutched his father to his chest. He had not passed out.

The stone had killed him.

Thank you for reading chapter one of GIFT OF THE PHOENIX. *You may purchase the novel at your favorite bookstore or online retailer.*

Learn more at DonnaCookAuthor.com

Connect with the Author

Sign up for updates at: donnacookauthor.com
Twitter @DonnaCookAuthor
Facebook.com/DonnaCookAuthor